CHRISTMAS
AT SADDLE CREEK

BOOKS BY SHELLEY PETERSON

The Saddle Creek Series

Dancer

Abby Malone

Stagestruck

Sundancer

Mystery at Saddle Creek

Dark Days at Saddle Creek

Jockey Girl

CHRISTMAS
AT SADDLE CREEK

Shelley Peterson

Cover image: shutterstock.com/horsemen
Printer: Webcom

Library and Archives Canada Cataloguing in Publication

Peterson, Shelley, 1952-, author
Christmas at Saddle Creek / Shelley Peterson.

(The Saddle Creek series)
Issued in print and electronic formats.
ISBN 978-1-4597-4026-6 (softcover).--ISBN 978-1-4597-4027-3 (PDF).--
ISBN 978-1-4597-4028-0 (EPUB)

I. Title. II. Series: Peterson, Shelley, 1952- . Saddle Creek series

PS8581.E8417C47 2017 jC813'.54 C2017-904773-6
C2017-904774-4

1 2 3 4 5 21 20 19 18 17

Conseil des Arts du Canada
Canada Council for the Arts

We acknowledge the support of the **Canada Council for the Arts**, which last year invested $153 million to bring the arts to Canadians throughout the country, and the **Ontario Arts Council** for our publishing program. We also acknowledge the financial support of the **Government of Ontario**, through the **Ontario Book Publishing Tax Credit** and the **Ontario Media Development Corporation**, and the **Government of Canada**.

Nous remercions le **Conseil des arts du Canada** de son soutien. L'an dernier, le Conseil a investi 153 millions de dollars pour mettre de l'art dans la vie des Canadiennes et des Canadiens de tout le pays.

Care has been taken to trace the ownership of copyright material used in this book. The author and the publisher welcome any information enabling them to rectify any references or credits in subsequent editions.

— J. Kirk Howard, President

The publisher is not responsible for websites or their content unless they are owned by the publisher.

Printed and bound in Canada.

VISIT US AT

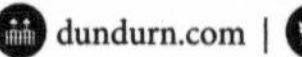
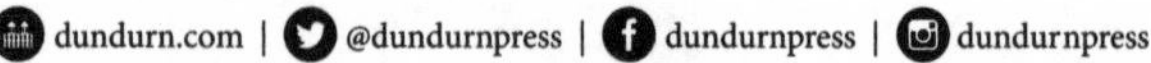

Dundurn
3 Church Street, Suite 500
Toronto, Ontario, Canada
M5E 1M2

To my own Cody — Wile E. Coyote — who was my watchful and loyal friend for eighteen years.

In memory of Laura Marie Peterson, who died October 10, 2015, and remains one of my most constant inspirations.

And to David, who loves Christmas more than anyone I know.

CHARACTERS

Bird: nickname for sixteen-year-old Alberta Simms.
Julia Simms: Bird's thirteen-year-old half-sister.
Eva Gilmour: Bird and Julia's mother; Hannah's younger sister.
Fred Sweetree: Bird's father; RCMP undercover officer.
Stuart Gilmour: Eva's new husband; principal of the local school.
Hannah Bradley: Bird's aunt; Eva's older sister; owns Saddle Creek Farm.
Dr. Paul Daniels: veterinarian; Hannah's fiancé.
Alec Daniels: son of Paul; boyfriend of Bird.
Jean Bradley: Bird's grandmother; Eva and Hannah's mother.
Kenneth Bradley: Jean's ex-husband; father of Eva and Hannah; grandfather of Bird and Julia.
Laura Pierson: friend of the family; lives at Merry Fields Farm.
Cliff Jones: Saddle Creek Farm manager.
Hilary James: "Mousie"; Dancer's owner; mother of Luke and Henry.
Joy Featherstone: Hilary's grandmother.
Sundancer: Bird's chestnut gelding; son of Dancer.
Cody: loyal wild coyote.
Lucky: Paul and Hannah's dog.

SADDLE CREEK FARM

1 BACK AT SADDLE CREEK FARM

'Twas the night before Christmas ...

Alberta Simms awoke with a start. Her eyes flew open to a wall of blackness. The cozy bedroom overlooking the front field at Saddle Creek Farm was totally dark, and apart from the steady pinging of freezing rain on the windowpanes, totally silent.

Her cellphone read 11:33 p.m.

What woke me up this time of night? she wondered. She slipped out from under her warm covers, and her bare feet felt the cold of the old pine as they touched the floor. She padded the two small steps to the window, pulled open the curtains, and peered outside into the darkness.

Alberta Simms was known by her nickname, "Bird." At sixteen, she was still slight and sinewy, but rapidly changing from girl to woman. Her skin was the colour of caffe latte, her eyes were a deep chocolate brown, and she wore her shiny dark hair long and loose. Bird was proud to be First Nations, and she looked far more like her First Nations father than her blond, blue-eyed mother of British heritage.

Her eyes began to adjust to the murkiness outside, and with effort she could make out the line of split-rail fencing that followed the laneway. Through the hail and fog she could see the three big maples on the lawn. One stood right in front of the house beside her window, and the others were on either side of the front walk. They looked blurry, but their forms were recognizable.

She could identify nothing that might have awoken her from her sleep.

Tonight was Christmas Eve. Tomorrow was Christmas. So far, her sixteenth Christmas was shaping up to be just like the fifteen that came before — full of disappointment and stress.

Her mother, Eva, was throwing hissy fits and bickering with her latest husband, Stuart. Bird and her little sister Julia joked that "Eva stole Christmas." But it was true. How much fun is it when somebody in the family is miserable and brings everybody's spirits down? No fun at all.

Bird groaned as she replayed this week's scene. Eva, with her face red and streaked with mascara, clothes strewn all over her bed and floor, whined that she didn't have anything to wear to Stuart's annual Christmas party. In Bird's opinion, Eva was right. Nothing in those rumpled piles suited her. She should throw out all the ribbons and bows and flouncy short skirts. It was embarrassing. Add overbleached, overcurled, long blond hair, plus too much makeup, and Eva looked like a cheap, wrinkly teenager trying out for the 1980 high school cheerleading team.

But she shouldn't have said it out loud.

Here was yet another example of how living with elective mutism can be an advantage. It was a horrible, frustrating affliction, and it had caused her untold misery, but when Bird was not able to speak, she never had to watch what she said.

Bird had been misdiagnosed with autism when she stopped speaking at age six. She was not typical in most ways, with her unusual ability to communicate non-verbally with animals, so it must have been difficult for the doctors, she conceded. But they got it right when they landed on a diagnosis of elective mutism. Her vocal cords worked just fine, but she couldn't get the words out of her mouth.

Now the words could come out, and her mother had not taken kindly to being called a 1980 vintage, wrinkly teenager. She "thought it best" that Bird stay with Aunt Hannah over Christmas. So Bird had been dumped unceremoniously at Saddle Creek, while thirteen-year-old Julia stayed with Eva. And now, instead of coming to Aunt Hannah's for Christmas, they were going to Stuart's parents' cottage in Muskoka for a big family gathering. Bird pictured an ornate tree, succulent turkey, lavish gifts, and joyful people hugging each other and laughing. But not with me, Bird thought. She sniffed back the aching feeling of hurt.

It wasn't news that Eva loved Julia more than she loved Bird. Julia was far more lovable, Bird admitted, and a blue-eyed blonde like Eva, of which their mother made a big deal. Bird didn't miss all the fuss and anxiety that accompanied Eva, but she wished that she could at least spend Christmas with her half-sister.

Bird curled her feet and stood on their outer edges to avoid the coldness of the floor. She was shivering but stayed for another minute at the window, just in case she'd missed something that might explain her disrupted sleep.

She had actually been looking forward to the Christmas celebration this year, but what had started out to be a decent-size dinner at Saddle Creek Farm had dwindled down to four people: Aunt Hannah, her veterinarian fiancé, Paul Daniels, Bird, and her grandmother, Jean Bradley. Not exactly a barrel of monkeys. Now it would be a very small gathering, with a very small turkey.

The real blow was Alec, who was now spending Christmas with his mother, which Bird understood completely. But having Alec there for dinner would've made everything great, even if nobody else came. She sighed deeply.

During those times when Bird couldn't talk and acted out in abnormal ways, Alec had been there for her. Everybody in the entire world thought she was a weirdo misfit, but Alec had always stood up for her. Bird smiled as she remembered how he used to translate for her when she couldn't speak, and how he'd faced down bullies at school when they were cruel.

They'd had a crush on each other for the last few years.

But now, things had changed. His father and her Aunt Hannah were engaged, and Bird wondered if their relationship might be too awkward. She wasn't sure how it would work at family get-togethers, like Christmas, which were always difficult, anyway. Alec refused to think there was a problem, but Bird had told him that they should talk about it, and until it was resolved one way or the other, at least they could remain friends.

Friends can't kiss each other, she thought. That might be difficult for her. Wow. Talk about confused emotions. Anyway, he wasn't coming for Christmas dinner so it wouldn't come up, but she was disappointed. Very.

She willed herself to focus on happy things. She loved being here at Saddle Creek with Aunt Hannah, Paul Daniels, and their funny brown dog, Lucky. She loved her cheerful little room in the farmhouse, with red, blue, green, and white tartan curtains and matching bedspread, and lively red sheets. She loved her interactions with Cody, the enigmatic coyote who appeared on a whim, or whenever he was needed, and disappeared again just as mysteriously. He'd been around for as long as she could remember.

More than anything else, she loved being with Sundancer, an undisputed jumping champion and her best friend. He was an athletic chestnut gelding who jumped anything that Bird faced him with and in stellar style. They'd had many adventures together, and they usually came home from competitions with trophies and ribbons galore.

There was never enough time to be around horses, she thought. Sunny gobbled up all her attention and still wanted more. Since arriving, Bird had done nothing much other than ride him, clean tack, and help muck out stalls, which was just how she liked it. If she could choose any place on Earth to be at any given moment, it would be right where she was now.

At Saddle Creek, Aunt Hannah unfailingly made her feel welcome and appreciated. She was kind and cheerful, and she made sure that Bird was looked after in every way. Like a mother might, thought Bird wistfully.

Aunt Hannah was nothing like her sister, Eva, and nothing like their father — Bird's grandfather — Kenneth Bradley, either. He was in jail for a variety of crimes, including insurance fraud, obstruction of justice, and collusion. He was plain bad. Bird briefly wondered what Christmas was like in jail. It wouldn't be great, but somehow she couldn't summon up sympathy for her grandfather. She'd been the recipient of his callous schemes on more than one occasion, including the time he'd sold Sundancer behind her back, with forged papers and false identity. He'd proven too many times how heartless he was, even setting up his mentally ill son, Tanbark Wedger, to take the blame for assault causing death. Bird didn't trust him one inch.

One day, Bird mused, she'd figure out the family dynamic. Why was Grandma Jean, his ex-wife, so ruined?

She'd been a beautiful, accomplished woman when he married her, at least judging from the old pictures. Now she was a prim, sarcastic, aloof alcoholic. And why were Kenneth's daughters both so strange around him? Aunt Hannah exhibited a forced cheerfulness and an agitated busyness whenever they were in the same house. And Bird's mother, Eva, became sickeningly girlish. Bird couldn't stand how she almost seemed to flirt with him.

Kenneth Bradley certainly casts a nasty spell on the people around him, she thought.

Suddenly, there was an ear-splintering crash right outside the window. Bird leapt back and landed on her bed.

A huge branch off the ancient maple that stood in front of the house broke from the tree and fell to the ground. It screeched as it scraped across the window and crash-landed on to the icy surface below. The noise was deafening.

Well, that's that, thought Bird. Mystery solved. I must've been awakened when the branch first began to crack.

By now, she was thoroughly chilled and needed to get some sleep. Tomorrow was Christmas, for better or for worse. She curled back up under her covers, bunched up the pillow until it was just right, and closed her eyes.

Bird took some deep, relaxing breaths. It really was good to be back at Saddle Creek Farm. Not good to be dumped here by her mother, but good to be here.

Her mind drifted as she sought out a comfortable sleeping pose. She wondered where her father, Fred Sweetree, would spend Christmas. Together, they'd solved the mystery of the lost, stolen, and murdered horses. They'd made a great team. Both shared the highly unusual ability of direct animal communication, and they could speak to each other telepathically, as well. Needless to say, as they figured out the case and caught the perpetrators, this talent had come in handy.

But as soon as the case was wrapped up, he was gone. Bird had just begun to know him a little and was feeling hopeful that she finally had a father. And not just any father. This father understood her, and he spoke to animals, just like her. He was caring and smart and honourable, plus a superb rider. He was a father she would love to spend time with. Bird felt a catch in her throat. It was not to be.

She'd last spoken to him at Pete Pierson's funeral. He'd told her he was proud of her and that he loved her, but he couldn't stay and be the kind of father that she wanted. Bird had no choice but to accept that, but still, it didn't totally sit right with her.

Her mother, Eva, never spoke of him. She'd always told Bird that he was dead. In fairness, everybody thought he'd died in a plane crash, so she couldn't blame Eva entirely. There was enough she could blame Eva for without adding that.

Bird pushed these troublesome thoughts away. She was tired and needed sleep. She stretched her entire body from the tips of her fingers to the ends of her toes, then loosened her muscles.

Bird let gravity pull her body into the mattress, and she asked her mind to float to a happy place. She imagined taking Sundancer out for a ride the next morning, after breakfast. The storm would have passed by then, the ice on the branches would be glistening in the sun, creating a fairy-tale world where everything was beautiful and full of goodness and light....

Bird girl.

Bird opened an eye.

Bird girl. You need to come. It was Cody.

What's wrong?

Just come. I'll show you the way.

Can it wait?

I think not.

The urgency in the coyote's telepathic transmission moved Bird to get back out from under the warmth of the quilts. Cody would not summon her unless it were serious.

Quickly she pulled on the jeans and sweater draped on the chair in the corner of the room. She began to tiptoe down the stairs, but stopped. Her phone. She might need it. She went back, grabbed her cell, and sped as quietly as she could to the kitchen. Bird threw on her coat and hat, stuffed her feet into her winter boots, and grabbed her sheepskin gloves.

Lucky appeared beside her, with his tail wagging madly. He sniffed her jeans. *Going out? Going out?*

Good dog, Lucky. Bird took a second to scratch his furry brown ears. *I need to go out for a while. You stay here.*

Lucky's tail stopped wagging.

You must guard the house, Lucky.

Lucky was confused. *I will come! Will come!*

Bird didn't know what Cody had in mind, and she didn't want to worry about Lucky in the storm. *Stay, Lucky. Hannah and Paul need you tonight. Guard them very well.*

Yes, Bird! Yes, Bird! His tail began to wag again.

Good dog, Lucky. I'll be back.

Bird watched him lie back down contentedly in his bed. He was a good dog, she thought. He always wanted to help. She opened the kitchen door to a blast of chilled air.

Oops, Bird remembered. Aunt Hannah would be mad if she woke up and didn't know where Bird was. It had happened before, and Bird had promised her that it'd never happen again.

She closed the door against the wind, spied the pen and pad of paper on the telephone desk under the clock, and scrawled, "Back soon. Call my cell. xo"

She glanced up at the clock. It was almost midnight.

Bird opened the door again and stepped outside. Stinging ice pellets hit her cheeks. She pulled her turtleneck collar over her nose and looked around for Cody.

Here, Bird girl. Follow me.

The coyote appeared from under a bush that sagged to the ground under a burden of ice. Cody looked thinner. Even in the dim light, she could see that his coat was dull. He walked toward her with a stiff gait.

Cody, are you all right?

Yes, Bird girl. We must hurry.

She'd ask Paul to take a look at him. *Where are we going?*

To the Good Lady's farm.

Cody called Laura Pierson "the Good Lady." She was quite elderly. Her husband, Pete, had died the year before. Cody had called him, "the Good Man." Now Mrs. Pierson lived alone on their farm called Merry Fields, just down the road.

That's a really long walk in this storm, Cody.

She needs help. Now.

What's wrong?

I must show you.

I'll get Hannah. We'll drive. Bird turned to go back into the house.

No! The road cannot let a car pass.

What? Sometimes it was hard to understand what Cody meant.

There is a big tree where a car would travel.

Oh.

Come with me, now!

Bird thought for a second. If Mrs. Pierson was in danger, she needed to get there fast. It would take too long by foot, and it was too icy to ride a bike.

I'll get Sunny. He'll save us a lot of time.

If you wish. But hurry.

Bird began to run to the barn, but with her first step she slid on a thin cover of ice on the driveway and landed on her bottom. Ice was everywhere. Would Sundancer be able to get down the lane, let alone all the way to Mrs. Pierson's farm?

She tested the thickness of the ice on top of the snow on the side by thumping it with her heel. She found she could break it easily. No problem for a horse's hooves to cut through the ice, she thought, but there was only one way to find out.

Bird very carefully made her way up the edge of the driveway to the barn and pulled open the door. She felt along the wall for the light switch and flicked it on.

Nothing but darkness. The power was out.

Bird stood in the middle of the aisle. Sundancer's stall was two down on the right.

Sunny?

Is that Santa Claus already?

It's me. I need your help.

You've got to be kidding.

Cody says Mrs. Pierson is in danger.

I'm waiting for Santa. It's cold and dark and scary out there. It's nighttime, and I want to sleep like all the other horses.

Those are a lot of excuses.

Another voice reached Bird.

I'll help! It was Tall Sox. *You helped me, and I'll help you anytime you ask.*

Thank you, Sox!

Amigo piped up. *Anything you ask, it is my duty.*

And me. I'll help you! The transmission came from Charlie, the old black gelding. *I'm ready to go!*

You are the best. Thank you, Sox, Amigo, and Charlie.

Sunny piped in. *No way! If any horse helps Bird, it's me. Get me outta this stall!*

Bird chuckled to herself. Just like Sundancer. She felt along the wall until she got to his stall. She grabbed his halter from its hook, opened the latch, and stepped inside with her arms out, feeling for her horse. He stood at the very back of the stall, making her go the whole way.

Got you. We're going to do it the quick way, Sunny. No time for tack. Your stable blanket stays on.

This better be worthwhile. A horse needs his sleep.

She put his halter over his head, fastened a rope to either side of it to make reins, then led him outside. She slid the door closed as she messaged to the barn filled with curious horses, *Good night, all. We have a job to do, but we'll be back soon.*

Bird led him to the mounting block outside the barn door and scrambled onto his back. *Be very careful, Sunny. It's icy.*

You don't say.

Take a step and see ...

They slid several feet until Sundancer found a snow bank where he could get purchase.

So, what's the plan, Bird? Skate until I break all my legs?

I thought your hooves would go through the ice and get a grip on the snow.

Because snow isn't slippery? Really?

Look, smarty, we need to help Mrs. Pierson. You don't like my ideas, so do you have any of your own?

It wasn't my idea to do this at all!

Okay, okay. Can we try to go cross-country?

Let me try it off the driveway. If it's bad, I'm not going. Sunny trod slowly and cautiously until he got to the edge of the lane, then stepped over the ice-encrusted bank onto the flat expanse of the field. His hooves cut through the thin layer of ice, and he relaxed. *Much better.*

Good, Sunny! Can we do this?

Just watch me.

Good boy!

I'm not a dog.

Sorry.

Sunny walked a few paces. The snow was heavy and deep. He had to bend his knees high to pick up his hooves before putting them down squarely again.

Not nice, Bird. Not nice at all.

But is it possible?

Possible, but every step is tough work. Sunny picked up a slow, high-stepping trot across the paddock to the gate into the woods. Bird kicked the ice off the latch and opened it, glad that the gate was hung high enough off the ground to be clear of the snow.

Once through the gate, they walked attentively along the trails. On top of the treacherous footing, it was pitch-dark. She longed to hurry, but if Bird were to be any help at all to Mrs. Pierson, she'd have to get to Merry Fields in one piece.

She noted that the conical shape of the fir trees on either side of the path allowed the snow and ice to slide off without breaking branches. Deciduous trees, like the big maple outside Bird's window, had the opposite shape and split with too much extra weight. Interesting, thought Bird.

These firs sheltered the trail from the full force of the gale, and as Bird and Sunny travelled along, they were glad for all the protection they could get.

By the time they emerged from the woods, Sundancer was sweating. Each step had been a big effort. They crossed a narrow clearing and found themselves at the road.

Sunny's sides heaved. *This is no picnic.*

We don't have far to go from here, Sunny.

The road looks crazy.

Bird had to agree. Sleet was blowing almost horizontal by the force of the wind, and garbage from a rolling bin was gusting around like it was in an anti-gravity machine. Just as plastic bags, wrappers, and sheets of newspaper were about to make a landing, they were tossed up in the air again. A telephone pole was down, and tree branches littered the road like pick-up sticks. Worse, the surface was slick with ice.

Her gut dropped. *Sunny. This is bad.*

I'm not a quitter, but I can't step on that.

It's solid ice. Bird felt like crying. She knew that the temperature couldn't be much below freezing for this kind of storm, but she was cold. Ice frosted her eyelashes and stung her eyes. She was soaked to the skin, right through her coat. She could feel her feet, but just. And now, after all this effort and getting this close, it looked like they might have to turn around.

Sunny pawed the road, testing the footing. *What about the Good Lady, Bird? She never gave up on us.*

Innumerable times over the years, Laura Pierson had helped them when they'd needed it. She was a person who could be counted on in every circumstance. Mrs. Pierson needed help, and they were very close. It was just a question of how.

Okay, Sunny, how do we get across?

I'll stay on this side of the road until I see a way.

Do you want me to get off?

No, not yet. You're keeping my back warm.

2 MERRY FIELDS

... And forth they went together,
Through the rude wind's loud lament
And the bitter weather.

Horse and girl walked on, heads bent against the fierce wind. Bird looked around. She hadn't seen Cody since they'd left the farm. He'd been right behind them when they went through the gate. *Cody? Where are you?*

There was no answer.

Sunny, have you seen Cody?

No. I don't feel his presence.

Bird began to worry. The small coyote had looked much frailer than before, and now he was somewhere out in this storm. Maybe Cody, the one who always helped others, needed help himself.

Cody? she messaged again. No reply.

Cody would show up, she told herself. He always does. She tried not to fret as she looked for familiar landmarks. Under normal conditions, Merry Fields should have been visible from there. In fact, Bird could've sworn it was almost across the road from the path they'd been on. But tonight, everything looked strange.

Bird! transmitted Sundancer. *I can get across here.*

Piles of withered leaves and sticks were scattered on the road, possibly from upended garbage cans. The horse stepped over the icy snow bank and used the discarded foliage as a path.

Good call, Sunny. We must be really close.

Are you kidding? We're here.

What? Bird was surprised to recognize the white mailbox that stood at the end of the Piersons' laneway. MERRY FIELDS 19347 was painted on it in dark green.

I would've walked right past it!

Duh. That's why you're the passenger.

You think you're so smart.

Smarter than you.

Aside from the mailbox, nothing else looked the same. The lane was totally obscured by ice-laden branches. The old willows on the front lawn bore no resemblance to their majestic past, and the birches at the side of the house had been demolished.

As they got closer, Bird saw a bigger problem.

The huge trembling aspen outside the kitchen door had split, and a big branch had come right through the roof of the porch. Another had fallen across the stairs.

Holy, she said. *This looks bad.*

Bird slid down from Sunny's back and promptly slipped on the ice.

See? Not as easy as you think.

Very true. Ouch. Stay here while I check out the house. Don't go far. I might need you.

You're very welcome.

Sorry. Thank you, Sunny. You did great. Really.

The big gelding snorted and stamped his feet. His mane was completely encrusted with icy strings. It made a jingly noise as he shook his neck. *I'll be in the shed, out of the wind.*

Okay.

Bird crouched over, prepared to break a fall as she slid one foot, then the other, across the ice to the farmhouse. She stepped over scattered branches and then climbed over the huge branch of the aspen to reach the door.

It was wide open. The house was very dark inside and just as cold as outdoors.

"Mrs. Pierson?" she called. She crossed the threshold cautiously and stood at the door frame. She called again, more loudly. "Mrs. Pierson? Are you here?"

Bird heard a weak cough from the corner, then another. She shuffled toward the noise with her arms outstretched, feeling her way. The floor was almost as slippery as the ice outside.

"Is that you, Bird?" croaked a thin voice.

Bird jumped out of her skin. "Mrs. Pierson? You scared me! Are you all right?"

"Not really, dear. I fell down. Can you find the flashlight for me, dear? It's in the cupboard beside the coat closet in the hall."

"Yes. I'll get it." Bird turned around and felt along the wall until she got to the hall. After a minute of uncertainty, she found a doorknob and opened what she hoped was the closet door. "Mrs. Pierson? Can you give me a clue? Which shelf?"

"I think it's on the top shelf over on the right. If not, the second from the top."

Bird reached up and felt around, unsure of what she was searching for, and at a great disadvantage in the dark. "Is it a big, square flashlight or ..." Bird's fumbling knocked things over and caused several objects to crash to the floor. "Sorry!"

"I think I heard it. Feel around on the ground."

"Okay." Bird got down on her knees and patted the floor until she felt a long, heavy cylinder with a large, round end. "Found it!"

She pressed a raised button. Light shone out in a steady beam, giving the room definition.

"This is great!" Bird exclaimed. She came back into the kitchen and took a good look.

"Oh, no. This is terrible."

The kitchen door was knocked right off its hinges. Not only had the branch broken through the porch, but it had also crashed through the kitchen wall.

The temperature was frigid inside the room, and sleet was blowing in through the opening and all across the floor. That's what's making it so slippery, Bird thought. And there was no way to keep out the elements. She quickly closed the hall door behind her in an effort to keep the cold from spreading throughout the rest of the house, realizing it was already too late.

The worst sight of all was when the flashlight lit up Laura Pierson. She was lying on the floor, shivering in her nightgown and slippers, looking very small and cold and dishevelled. Her back was hunched against the wall, her bare, blue-veined legs were out straight, and one ankle was quite swollen. Her old face was pale, her puffy white hair was askew, and her glasses had smashed on the floor beside her, leaving her small blue eyes squinting and blinking against the light. A trickle of blood seeped from the bridge of her nose. Her forehead was bruised.

"What happened?" asked Bird. "How long have you been sitting here? And where do you hurt?"

"Can you get me that blanket, dear? The one on the chair?"

Bird took the plaid wool throw off the back of the armchair next to the fireplace and gently wrapped it around the old lady's shoulders, then grabbed another blanket from the couch and put it over her legs.

"Be careful of my ankle, dear. I'm feeling rather vulnerable."

Bird nodded. "You can't stay here in the cold. I'll call 911."

"Yes. Please do that, dear. I need some water."

Bird stood up, pulled her cell from her pocket, and punched in the three numbers. She placed the flashlight end-up on the floor to illuminate the entire room. As she waited for an operator to answer, she brought over a glass of water from the sink.

Mrs. Pierson drank it down and motioned for Bird to refill it.

Bird filled the glass again at the sink. The water pressure was lessening. Bird knew that pumps don't work without power, and once the previously pumped water was gone, there'd be no more until the power came back on.

She gave the water to Mrs. Pierson and waited while she drained the glass, then refilled it. Good thing Cody had come to get her when he did.

Again, Bird wondered if the coyote was okay.

The call went to a recorded message, asking Bird to be patient because of an extraordinary number of emergency calls, and informing her that her call would be answered in sequence. She was asked to press one for police, two for fire, and three for an ambulance. Bird pressed three. Another recorded message asked that she be patient because of an extraordinary number of emergency calls, and informed her that her call would be answered in sequence.

Bird willed herself to stay calm. How can I be patient at a time like this? she wondered.

She thought about hanging up and calling Paul and Hannah. But the roads were impassable. They couldn't come to help, and she'd only make them worry. They'd wake up and not get back to sleep, and for nothing.

Holding her cellphone to her ear, she checked out the oddly tilted kitchen door. She made an effort to get it closed but had no luck. The weight of the tree on the door frame was enormous.

How could she stop the continuous flow of cold air and sleet? The pipes would freeze. Bird opened the old wooden trunk next to the armchair and found a thick grey army blanket.

"Can I nail this up, Mrs. Pierson?"

The old woman nodded feebly. She was losing energy.

Bird was still on hold. She put her phone on speaker and set it on the table while she found some nails and a hammer in the hall closet, then tacked up the blanket. She put a pile of books on the blanket edge, which kept it from flapping in the wind. With the wind blocked, suddenly there was quiet. It was a bigger relief than Bird expected.

Mrs. Pierson was asleep. Bird hoped that she hadn't fainted.

Finally, a male operator answered. "This is 911. What is your emergency?"

Bird scrambled for the phone and said, "My name is Alberta Simms. I'm at the farm of Laura Pierson at 19347 Third Line, Caledon. I'm her neighbour. She's in her nineties. She's hurt and needs help."

There was a pause. "The third line of Caledon, north of the Grange, is completely blocked at this time. The hydro lines are down. No emergency vehicles are able to pass, and they will not be able to reach you until the hydro crews clear the roads of danger. What is the nature of her injury?"

Bird assessed Mrs. Pierson. She looked terrible, even worse than before. "A tree fell on her house. She's lying on the floor, and she's either asleep or unconscious. There's a bump growing on her forehead. Her right ankle is twice as big as her left."

The man asked, "Can you make her comfortable?"

Bird grimaced. "I'm not sure. She's in a lot of pain."

"Raise her injured ankle so it rests above her heart, keep her hydrated, and if there's Tylenol, give her three tablets. Do not give her Aspirin because it's a blood thinner. And try to keep her body warm any way you can."

"Okay. How soon do you think somebody will come? The house is freezing, and she's really old."

"An ambulance will arrive at the earliest possible time, but it might be several hours. I've put in a request. That's all I can do. Please continue to do what you can for her, and we will get to her as soon as possible."

"I'll do my best. Thank you."

"Can I reach you at this number?"

"Yes."

"Good. We'll call with an update as soon as we can."

"Okay. I hope it's soon."

"Good luck, Bertha."

Bird pressed "end," suddenly very unsure of what to do. Would Mrs. Pierson be okay for several hours? She understood their problem with the hydro lines down, but could the old woman survive this cold and the pain in her ankle, and maybe a concussion, for much longer?

The way Bird saw it, Mrs. Pierson likely slipped on the icy floor when she got out of bed to investigate the crash in her kitchen. Bird calculated how long she'd been lying there. Cody had woken Bird just before midnight. It would've taken Cody at least twenty minutes to get from Merry Fields to Saddle Creek Farm, so he left to get help around 11:30 p.m. Bird's cellphone read 1:36 a.m., so Mrs. Pierson had been sitting on the floor for at least a couple of hours, plus however long she'd been there before Cody noticed. How much longer could they wait?

Bird knelt at the woman's side. "Mrs. Pierson?"

She didn't respond. Bird gently shook her shoulder.

Laura Pierson groaned quietly and let out a tiny cough, like the one Bird heard when she first entered the house.

Bird stood up. She made her decision. Mrs. Pierson could not wait until the hydro lines had been cleared. She needed to come home to Saddle Creek now, and Bird had a plan.

She picked up the flashlight, walked to the washroom, and looked behind the sink mirror and in all the drawers for the drugs that the man had prescribed. None. Bird ran upstairs and checked the bedroom and cupboards. Finally, she found a bottle of Tylenol. It had expired six years ago, but Bird deemed it would be better than nothing.

She came downstairs, was able to fill the water glass one more time, and urged Mrs. Pierson to take the pills, which was very difficult for her because while she could briefly open her eyes, she was still not anywhere near alert. Instead of three tablets, Bird gave her four. Whatever strength they had left, Mrs. Pierson would need.

Bird? Are you in there? What's taking so long? Her horse stretched his neck and pushed the blanket over the door with his nose, causing it to come away from one of the nails.

Sunny! I was just coming to get you.

Can we go home? I want to go back to my stall.

Yes, we can, but we're taking Mrs. Pierson with us.

That's crazy. She's too old to learn to ride.

We're going to pull her in a sled.

We're going to pull her? Or I'm *going to pull her?*

You're going to pull her.

What's in it for me?

You go home to your stall.

Done.

First, I need to find a sled.

What's that?

A flat piece of wood that people slide down hills on.

Hey! There's one in the shed, where I've been waiting forever and ever.

Great! Are there ropes in there, too?

There are metal ropes.

Chains? I'll go look.

Bird took another look at Mrs. Pierson. A large bruise was forming on the bump that was growing on her forehead. Bird noted how transparent skin gets as people age, and she worried again about a concussion. She hurried outside with the flashlight.

She was relieved to find that the wind had died down, which made the night feel warmer, and the icy rain had stopped. Thankfully, the moon was beginning to show through the cloud cover. With much better visibility, things boded well for the trip back to Saddle Creek. At least there was some good news in the pile of bad.

Bird followed Sunny to the shed beside the house. A fresh pile of manure indicated where her horse had sheltered.

Just as Sunny had said, an old wooden toboggan was hanging on the far wall. The front was curled up so it could slide through snow, and the end had a back support so kids wouldn't fall off. There were green cushions nailed on, and it was long enough for several children to go for a ride down a hill. Long enough to pull Mrs. Pierson to Saddle Creek. It looked homemade. Bird felt sure that Mr. Pierson had built it, and he'd be glad for it to be used to get his wife to safety. Mrs. Pierson had been the treasure of his life.

She lifted it off the wall and set it on the ground.

The chains that Sunny had mentioned were meant to pull trucks out of ditches and far too heavy for this job. She shone the light over the walls and along the shelves. Just when she was about to concede defeat, she noticed a blue plastic container behind some water barrels. She lifted the lid to find coils of rope covered with grease, probably from some machine. They would do perfectly.

Bird threw the ropes on the sled and pulled it over the branches and into the kitchen. After briefly thinking about the best way Mrs. Pierson should travel, she decided that feet first might be easier. She took some cushions off the couch and laid them on the sled. She put two throw pillows at the back for Mrs. Pierson's head and neck, and a third pillow at the front for the swollen ankle to be raised.

Now she uncoiled the soiled ropes and figured out how to fit them on Sundancer so he could pull the sled. With kitchen shears from a drawer, she cut a length to be used around his rib cage, just behind his front legs. She cut another to hang around his neck, and another to form loops to run the rope through, which would attach to the sled.

Mrs. Pierson groaned. Bird glanced at her and noticed that her skin had turned almost blue. There was no time to waste. Bird ducked under the hanging blanket and, once outside, fastened the ropes onto Sunny like a harness.

These ropes stink.

They're the only ones we have. And they're on top of your blanket so they mostly don't touch you.

The horse snorted and pawed the ground. *Hurry up, then.*

She fed another, longer rope through the loop on his left side, across his chest, supported by the loose rope around his neck so it wouldn't slip down over his front legs, and back again through the loop on his right. Both ends of that rope would fasten the sled to the horse. She studied her work and was satisfied.

This rope on my chest? It's going to rub the fur right off my shoulders.

Through your blanket?

Yes, through my blanket. Too much pressure on one spot.

If you insist. Bird dashed back to the kitchen and grabbed two dishtowels. She wrapped them around the sections of rope that came into contact with the gelding's shoulders. *Better?*

Maybe.

Okay, I'm going to get Mrs. Pierson on the sled. Don't move, or these ropes will get all tangled up in your legs.

This is not how I imagined spending Christmas.

Dream of all the bran mash you can eat.

Promise?

Promise. I couldn't do this without you. She patted her horse's nose. *Really.*

Sunny put his head against her chest. He was pleased.

Bird ducked back under the blanket over the door, into the kitchen. She pulled the sled as close to the woman as she could get. "Mrs. Pierson, can you help me?"

The old woman opened one eye and blinked. She coughed again and began to shiver. "Bird? What are you doing here? Where am I?"

"You're lying on your kitchen floor, and you've been hurt. We have to get to Saddle Creek. You'll freeze if you stay here. Your ankle is swollen, and you might have bonked your head."

"I did, dear. I did bonk my head. It hurts," she said weakly.

"I'm so sorry."

"It's not your fault, dear."

Bird was touched that, even in pain, Mrs. Pierson was considerate of her feelings. "Can you slide your body over a little, onto the sled?"

"I'm very cold, dear. Can you bring me another blanket?"

"Yes, I'll wrap you right up." Bird ran to the hall closet, and she found a long, down-filled red coat, a padded hat with earflaps, big plaid mittens, and some old fleece-lined boots that had belonged to Mr. Pierson. Mrs. Pierson hadn't had the heart to throw his stuff out, thought Bird. And a good thing, too.

Mrs. Pierson was as helpful as possible as Bird dressed her. She tried not to whimper when the big boot was pulled over her ankle, but cried out in pain when Bird began to move her onto the sled.

"Ooooh. Sorry, dear! Owwww. Oh, sorry. Ahhhhhh!"

"You're doing great, Mrs. Pierson. Just a couple more inches, and you're on. Great! Good work!"

"Oh-oh-oh-oh-oh-oh!"

"You did it!"

Mrs. Pierson was now on the sled. Bird poured the last of the water from her glass into a thermos and put it at her feet, along with the flashlight, and then checked the cushions to make sure that her precious patient would be as comfortable as possible.

Bird saw a problem. Mrs. Pierson could roll off. Not good. She cut a long length of rope and wound it tightly twice around the entire circumference of the sled. She used the curl on the front and the backrest on the rear to secure it, successfully fashioning a railing made of rope. It would have to do.

Ah, Bird?

I didn't forget you, Sunny. We're ready to go. Can you back up to the porch?

Righto.

He backed up as close as he could get, straddling the thick branch of the fallen tree.

Bird pulled down the grey army blanket that had been covering the door, and she carefully wrapped it around Mrs. Pierson. She took the ropes that she'd threaded through Sunny's makeshift harness and tied them through the front curl of the sled, then double-knotted them on the ropes that formed the railing.

Let's go home, Sunny.

Music to my ears.

3 CODY

Sire, the night is darker now,
And the wind blows stronger.
Fails my heart, I know not how.
I can go no longer.

Bird asked Sunny to inch ahead slowly until the sled had been pulled out of the house and through the shattered porch. The giant branch of the aspen lay across the two steps to the ground. To minimize the jolt, Bird held up the end of the sled and lifted it over. It was very heavy but she managed, just.

She walked beside the sled as they moved across the yard, toward the road. Mrs. Pierson hadn't moved.

Too slow. Sunny was impatient. *We'll never get home.*

I know, but the smoother, the better for Mrs. Pierson.

I can do smooth. Sunny picked up his pace very slightly.

Mrs. Pierson cried out each time they went over a bump, and with all the branches scattered around, there were many. Bird lifted the end of the sled as much as she could, trying to soften the impact. She flinched every time the woman moaned, in sympathy with her pain.

Bird began to second-guess her decision. *Are we doing the right thing, Sunny?*

How am I to know? I'm a horse.

You said you're smarter than me.

I was joking.

Should we wait for an ambulance to come?

How long?

I don't know. It might be several hours.

Then cut these ropes and let me go. I know the way.

Bird hated putting Mrs. Pierson through the rough ride, but an ambulance would be bumpy, too, and Mrs. Pierson couldn't wait much longer to get help. She was finished second-guessing. *Let's go home the way we came, Sunny.*

There's no other way.

Keep an eye out for Cody.

I've been looking for him all night.

Bird and Sundancer crossed the ice-covered road very carefully. To keep from slipping, Sunny needed to walk over the leaves and sticks, but even the slightest variance on the surface caused Laura Pierson to whimper.

Bird solved the problem by pulling the sled over the icy part of the road herself. She stepped between the horse and the sled, took the ropes in her hands, and moved over to the right. Sunny and Bird walked parallel to each other, allowing the sled to travel over the ice, and Sunny on the path of debris. It was much better, but far from perfect.

Their tension dissipated slightly once they reached the other side of the road and were on to firmer footing.

The moon was lighting up their way, the wind had abated, and the temperature was moderating. Bird counted their blessings. Still, pulling the sled with an elderly, injured person on board made the journey difficult and stressful, and within half an hour they both needed to stop.

Laura Pierson had stopped making noises fifteen minutes earlier. Bird checked to be sure she was alive, and she was happy to hear a feeble cough. She brought the thermos to her lips and tried to get her to drink. Mrs. Pierson took only a sip.

The big chestnut gelding stood with his head down. He was breathing heavily. Bird patted his neck. *You're doing great. We'll be home soon and can get some rest.*

I've ceased caring. I'll die out here.

Sunny! Don't make jokes like that.

I'm not joking.

Suddenly, the horse lifted his head. His upper lip flipped up, over his nostrils.

What is it? asked Bird.

It's Cody.

Where?

Very close.

But where? Why can you hear him and not me?

I smell him. The wind keeps changing, but he's somewhere over there. Sundancer motioned slightly to the left and ahead of them with his nose.

In the woods, off the path?

Yes.

You stay here with the sled, and I'll go look.

Bird took the flashlight from the toboggan and headed off in the direction Sunny had indicated. She shone the light under each bush and behind every rock. *Cody?* she transmitted. *Cody? Where are you? Please, please stay alive until I find you!*

Tears rolled down her face as she searched. She didn't want to give up, but Mrs. Pierson needed help. Bird made the decision to circle back to the sled. She hoped the coyote would turn up by the time she got back.

He hadn't.

Sunny, I can't find him. Can you still smell him?

Yes. He's close by. Try over there. The big gelding looked ahead and to his right this time.

Okay.

Bird shone the light on the right side of the path and kept walking. Sunny was moving along with her, in the direction of home. *Cody! Cody, where are you?*

Nothing came back to her. No sound at all, either by vocal cords or telepathic transmission. She closed her eyes and imagined the small coyote. A sudden emotional tug caused her to move a bit farther into the brush. She opened her eyes.

There. Pinned under a fallen branch. Was that a large lump of dirt or a mossy rock? It was the same size as the small coyote and coated with sleet.

Bird edged closer, ducking under cedars and shrubs, until she crouched beside it. She shone the light right at it. It was furry. It was an animal, for sure. And it looked dead.

Slowly she reached out a gloved hand and brushed the ice off the creature.

It reacted. Bird jumped back. It was alive, but what was it?

Very faintly, she got a transmission. *Bird girl.*

Cody! It's you!

Goodbye, Bird girl.

No! It's not time!

The other world is calling. I'm going to the western sky.

No, Cody, I'm taking you home with me.

With a great effort, Bird pushed the broken bough aside. She scooped him up as gently as she could. *Don't be upset with me, Cody. I can't leave you here.*

She protected him from the stinging branches with their hanging loads of ice and snow. She carried him close to her chest, intermittently walking backward and sideways and on her knees until they were back onto the path.

Sunny was there, waiting for them.

Cody's alive but barely. He was hit with a falling branch.

Bird lifted the blankets from Mrs. Pierson's legs and placed the coyote beside her.

Here, you'll stay warm, Cody, and you'll keep Mrs. Pierson warm, too. She's hurt and sick like you. She covered him up and tucked the blanket under the cushion so Cody wouldn't roll off.

The moon had now fully emerged from the clouds, and they were able to move on more quickly. Mrs. Pierson remained silent, and Cody didn't move. Many times, Bird almost stopped Sunny so she could check on them, but it was more important to keep going. There was nothing she could do for them, anyway.

By the time Sunny and Bird made their way through the gate at the far end of the Saddle Creek field, it was four o'clock in the morning. Finally, they'd returned with their precious load.

As they passed the barn, Bird asked, *Do you want me to untie you here? I can pull the sled to the house. It's downhill.*

No. I've come this far. I'm going all the way.

You are the best horse in the world.

Don't forget that.

Bird chuckled. She suddenly felt like laughing out loud, she was so happy to be home.

Keep it together, Bird.

You're right. We're so close I want to rush.

Together, they made their way to the front of the farmhouse and came to a stop. Bird threw a snowball at the window of Aunt Hannah's bedroom. Her aim was good.

Almost immediately, the upstairs window opened. Hannah stuck her head out the window.

"Bird? What the heck? What's going on?"

"We need help. Mrs. Pierson and Cody are both hurt. They're on the sled!"

Hannah looked astonished. She was about to say something but changed her mind and closed her mouth. The window slammed shut. In less than a minute, Hannah and Paul were outside.

As a veterinarian, Paul was accustomed to emergencies, and he immediately went into action mode, checking the injured woman and coyote before moving them.

Efficiently, Hannah prepared the couch. She held the door while Paul carried Mrs. Pierson into the house, utterly limp and emitting not a sound. Paul's mouth was drawn tightly, and he appeared very concerned.

Once Mrs. Pierson was safely inside, Bird lifted Cody out of the sled. She gingerly moved him to the kitchen.

Lucky wagged his tail. *He can have my bed! My bed!*

Thank you, Lucky. You're such a good dog. She placed Cody as gently as possible on Lucky's bed. He whimpered softly, which she took as a good sign. Lucky sat beside him, pleased to be of service. Bird smiled sleepily and patted his head.

"I'm going to put Sunny to bed now," she said. She could barely keep her eyes open. "Is there anything I can do for Mrs. Pierson? Or Cody?"

"Nothing, Bird. Leave them both to us. You go."

"I'll give Sunny a bran mash if he'll eat it."

Hannah nodded. "And put a dry blanket on him. Go, Bird. Get that good horse whatever he wants. I can't believe what you two have done tonight. We want to hear the whole story."

Bird's heart swelled with gratitude for her aunt's words of praise, and she felt hot tears on her cheeks. Now that the job was done, she felt all the energy drain from her body. She dragged herself outside again carrying a big pair of scissors.

Sunny, I'm going to cut these ropes off you, and you're going to bed.

I've never heard more beautiful words.

Bird had to muscle the scissors to cut away the rope harness, but soon Sunny was released. They left the toboggan and the bits of rope on the ground where they fell, and she and her horse trudged up the lane to the stable, side by side.

Do you want a mash tonight?

Too tired. Tomorrow, though, an extra big one.

Done.

Bird pulled off his wet blanket and hung it up on a hook to dry. She gave him two large flakes of hay, filled his water, and found some mints for him in the tack room. She took a clean towel and rubbed his coat from head to hoof, covered him with a clean stable blanket, and buckled it up.

The other horses were very curious about what had happened. Bird briefly explained: *Cody told us the Good Lady needed help. We brought her home with us. Cody had an accident so he's in the farmhouse, too, and Dr. Paul is fixing him up.*

Details tomorrow, Sunny added. *I need sleep.*

Merry Christmas, Sunny, messaged Bird. *We'll never forget this one.*

Sunny nickered sleepily. *Merry Christmas, Bird.*

Bird patted his neck and rubbed his ears. She left his stall and walked down the aisle to the door, then turned and messaged, *Merry Christmas to all, and to all a good night!*

Every horse but Sunny stomped and neighed and nodded in response. Sunny laid himself down and promptly fell asleep.

Bird returned to the house in a trance. She was so exhausted that when she removed her wet outer clothing and hung them up, she didn't notice when they fell to the floor.

Aunt Hannah was watching her. "Bird, you sweet thing. You get upstairs to bed. Sleep in as long as you can."

Bird nodded numbly. She climbed the stairs on her hands and knees, peeled off her wet clothes, and dropped into bed.

In seconds, she was dead to the world in the Land of Nod.

Bird was dreaming. Everything was beautiful. The sun was streaming through her open curtains, and there were winter birds chirping and singing and cheerfully bantering to each other. Cardinals, blue jays, and chickadees were in a marvellous, magical chorus, each outdoing the other to serenade this wondrous day.

She opened one eye. This was no dream. She hadn't bothered to close her curtains when she'd gone to bed, and light was pouring in. The birdsong was almost deafening.

She looked at the clock beside her bed. It was two o'clock in the afternoon.

Two o'clock, thought Bird. I've been sleeping for nine hours! She counted again. By the time she'd gotten to bed it was after five o'clock in the morning. Yes. Nine hours.

She stretched from head to toe. Her nose twitched. Something delicious was cooking downstairs, sending up aromas to call her from her bed. It wasn't bacon, but it was definitely appealing. Turkey? Of course, she thought. It's Christmas Day.

Christmas. Her stomach dropped. It was always such a disappointment.

Her mind cleared with a snap. What about Mrs. Pierson? And Cody? She'd fallen asleep without knowing if they'd be okay. And the last time she'd seen them, they'd both looked terrible.

Bird jumped out of bed. Her room felt unusually cold. She threw on a clean sweatsuit and slippers, ran down the stairs, and opened the door into the kitchen.

"Good morning, Bird, and Merry Christmas!" sang Aunt Hannah. She was peeling potatoes at the sink, and she looked ridiculous in a Santa hat and Christmas apron. She wore reindeer slippers and red striped socks that made her look like an aging elf.

"Close the hall door behind you?" she asked. "We're trying to keep this room warm."

"Okay." Bird did as she was told. "I slept forever! Where's Mrs. Pierson? Where's Cody?"

"Over here, you dear, dear girl," said Mrs. Pierson.

Bird twirled to face the old woman. She was on the

kitchen couch, nestled under layers of quilts. "You're alive! You look great! How are you feeling?"

"Aside from an ache where I banged my head and the pain in my ankle, which I stupidly twisted, I've never felt better." Mrs. Pierson smiled at Bird. Her bright blue eyes twinkled just like before. "You and your horse saved my life last night, dear. I really don't know how to thank you."

"It was Cody. He came to get me. I would never have known you were in trouble, otherwise. He's the one you should thank." Bird looked around the room for Cody. Lucky's bed was empty.

She turned to Hannah with dread in her heart. She had to ask. "Where's Cody?" she whispered.

Hannah grinned. Bird looked at her questioningly.

Mrs. Pierson answered. "Over here, dear." She lifted the top quilt. The old coyote was on the couch, cuddled up under the covers with the old lady.

Cody lifted his head and yawned. *Hello, Bird girl.*

Bird's eyebrows lifted. She was astonished. Cody was a wild animal. He hated being indoors. He hated being cuddled. He hated being close to people. She would never have imagined this sight in a million years.

"Why are you so surprised, Bird?" Mrs. Pierson's eyes twinkled with mischief. "Cody visited me in the hospital years ago and hid under the covers to escape capture. We're renewing our acquaintance."

Bird shook her head. "I never heard that story."

"Ask Abby Malone someday, dear. Cody and I go way back." She patted Cody's head softly. "It was when

I was trampled by Pete's cows." She grimaced with the memory.

Bird remembered hearing something about that. She'd ask later, but her concern at that moment was for Cody.

Cody? Are you okay?

I'm very old and very cold this winter. Warm now.

I'm glad.

I did not wish to be saved.

Are you happy now? To be alive?

Yes. I am beholden. The coyote put his head back under the quilt. *I have one more task to perform before I leave this place.*

One more task?

I know not what. Not yet.

Bird considered the coyote's words. She knew from experience that she would find out their meaning in time. Now the sight of Cody and Mrs. Pierson on the couch made her chuckle. "You two belong together."

Mrs. Pierson threw back her head and laughed. "I never wanted a dog. I didn't know I was waiting all my life for a coyote!"

Hannah was finished peeling the potatoes and began rinsing lettuce. "Oh, Bird, your cellphone was ringing while you were asleep. I let it go to voice mail, but it rang again so I picked it up."

"Who was it?"

"The Emergency operator. He wanted to speak to Bertha." She smiled at Bird and wiped her teary eyes with the back of her hand. "Onions. Anyway, the road is cleared. I told him not to worry about Mrs. Pierson, but to please get our power connected because we have people coming for Christmas dinner."

Bird was puzzled. The kitchen lights were on, and judging from the delicious aroma, the oven was cooking a turkey. "We don't have power?"

"Cliff hooked up his portable generator for us."

"That's nice," said Bird. Cliff was the farm manager and Hannah's valued right-hand man. "That leaves him in the cold."

"That's not all," said Mrs. Pierson. "He took the tractor over to my farm this morning and took the tree off my house. He got my kitchen door closed." She looked very pleased. "And he tarped the hole in the kitchen ceiling and drained the pipes so I don't have a flood. Cliff is a nice boy. I invited him to dinner."

"Great," said Bird. "Is his family coming?"

Hannah answered, "No, they can't get here because of the storm. Quite a few of the major roads are still closed." She glanced at the clock. "Bird, eat something now because dinner will be on the table before you know it, and I'll need some help."

"Sure! I'll grab a banana and go see how Sunny's doing."

"He's right outside in his field," said Hannah. "He looks no worse for wear."

"That Sundancer," smiled Mrs. Pierson. "I wish I'd been awake for the ride home in the sled. But then again, maybe it was better that I blacked out. The pain was horrible."

"You sure seem better this morning, Mrs. Pierson."

"I am, dear. Dr. Paul wrapped up my ankle and gave me some painkillers that work miracles." Her eyes twinkled with mischief. "I'm going to fire my doctor and get myself a vet."

From the look of her now, Bird wished she'd had some of Paul's drugs to give Mrs. Pierson on their trip home last night.

She went to the kitchen door and saw that her coat and boots were still wet. She borrowed Hannah's red jacket and boots, and went out to the field across from the house.

Sunny!

Hey, Bird. You look like Hannah. The big chestnut gelding ambled up to the fence. *You smell like her, too.*

And you look like Charlie. She patted his nose.

Cliff mixed up the blankets.

Thanks for helping last night.

You mean for suffering through a long and dangerous journey that could have ended in disaster?

I mean for saving a nice old lady and a nice old coyote from certain death.

I was happy to do it, Bird.

I was happy to do it, too.

But don't ask again too soon. That was hard work.

Agreed. I slept like a log.

Oh, Bird. Hannah left something for you on the gate.

There. Sunny looked over at a black cloth bag that was attached to the post with a long red ribbon.

What is it?

It's not food, that's all I know.

Bird snorted. If there'd been anything edible, the bag would not still be hanging untouched.

She opened it and pulled out a leather show bridle. It was the most beautifully made bridle that she'd ever seen. Bird took off her gloves and felt the softness of the leather, and she delighted in the hand-done stitching. The card read, "With love and pride, Aunt Hannah and Paul."

Sunny, now people will notice us when we enter the ring!

Ha. They do already. A little leather doesn't win a class.

It's still really nice.

Nice if you make it fit me just right, and as long as it doesn't get in the way of my brilliance.

Nothing can. I don't need to tell you, you're the best.

The horse rubbed his head affectionately on Bird's shoulder. She scratched him behind his ears. They stood silently for a few minutes, enjoying the peaceful companionship.

The silence was interrupted by the sound of a car bumping over ice. Girl and horse turned to look.

It was Stuart driving his Jeep up the driveway. Her mother, Eva, was glowering in the passenger seat and her sister, Julia, sat in the back.

What are they doing here? wondered Bird.

Julia began to wave madly when she saw Bird. As soon as the car stopped, she threw open the door and hopped out.

"Bird! Bird! We're here for Christmas! I'm so excited!" She ran to her big sister and gave her an enormous hug. "Merry Christmas!"

"Merry Christmas, Julia! This is a surprise!" Bird was elated to see Julia but had very mixed feelings about her mother, who after Bird's wrinkly cheerleader remark had made it abundantly clear that she was not a part of her Christmas.

Stuart carried two suitcases from the car. Grinning, he put one down to wave to Bird. Eva rushed past him into the house without a glance.

Merry Christmas to you, too, Mom, Bird thought.

"Does Aunt Hannah know you're coming?" she asked.

"Yeah, Mom called her this morning. Some of the roads are closed so we can't go to Stuart's family in Muskoka. Hooray! Didn't she tell you?"

"I just woke up so I guess lots of things have happened."

"You never sleep in. Are you sick?"

"No. It's a long story. I'll tell you all about it, but take in your bags. I have to go up to the barn and then I'll be right there."

"Okay," called Julia. She was already hopping and skipping to the car to get her things.

"Oh, Julia," called Bird. "Mrs. Pierson's on the couch with a sprained foot so don't jump on her."

She watched her little sister fondly. Julia always

brought cheerfulness wherever she went. Christmas was looking up.

Suddenly, in mid hop, the younger girl stopped. "Bird? This sled? And these hoofprints! Was Santa here?"

Bird laughed. "Of course Santa was here. You've been a very good girl. Ask Mrs. Pierson about it."

Sunny, did you think of that when you were pulling the sleigh last night, on Christmas Eve?

What?

That you were Rudolph the Red-Nosed Reindeer and Mrs. Pierson was Santa?

No.

I didn't, either.

But I did notice that I was born in a stable. The horse lifted his head and let out a whinny.

You think you're so funny. Bird laughed, then reached up to give him a rub behind one of his ears. *I promised you a bran mash. Let's go.*

A big one. You promised me a big *bran mash.*

And you will get it. You deserve it.

4 SURPRISE ARRIVALS

O Christmas tree, O Christmas tree ...

After hanging the new bridle in the tack room with care and giving Sunny his mash, Bird returned to the house from the barn. There were two men in the kitchen wearing heavy work coats. One was quite tall and thin, and the other was short and burly. They worked for the hydro company and had reconnected the lines on the road. They had dropped in to check if the power was back on.

"Are you sure you won't have a coffee?" Hannah asked.

"Maybe one for the road, if it's really no trouble. Double-double for both of us, thanks."

"How are the roads?"

"The crews are working around the clock," said the tall man. His name tag said Tom. "But nothing's moving north of here, and roads to the west are still a disaster."

The stocky man, Bob, added, "We've been at it all night."

Mrs. Pierson asked, "Have you had anything to eat, dears?"

The two men looked at each other, unsure of how to answer.

"You haven't, have you!" she declared. "Hannah, get these men a sandwich with their coffee!"

"And a beer," said Stuart, who'd just walked in from the hall. He pulled a chair from under the table and sat down. He appeared subdued to Bird.

"Can you stay for Christmas dinner?" asked Mrs. Pierson. "It'll be ready in just a couple of hours."

Bird smiled. Mrs. Pierson was always so welcoming, even in somebody else's house.

The men shook their heads simultaneously. Bob said, "That's mighty nice of you, but no can do. We've got a lot more ground to cover before the end of our shift."

"Come back, then," insisted Mrs. Pierson. "We'd be happy if you would. Wouldn't we, Hannah dear?"

Hannah was put on the spot. Bird could see her mentally counting how many more places could be set at the table.

Tom answered before Hannah could respond. "Well, thanks, but my wife is cooking up a storm, and that's where I'm headed after work. Bob here is the bachelor."

"A bachelor?" said Mrs. Pierson. "Hmm. I might have someone for you."

Bob blushed. "I'm a bachelor, but my good mother would cry if I miss her Christmas dinner."

"Bring your mother, too," said Mrs. Pierson. "And Tom, bring your family. All of them!"

Bird and Hannah looked at each other with amusement. Bird began to wonder if the drugs Paul had given Mrs. Pierson were a little strong.

"Here you go!" Hannah handed them two packed lunches.

"No beer?" Bob kidded.

"In the bottom of the bags, for after work. Coke for now." Hannah wagged her finger at him and grinned.

Bob gave her a business card. "Thanks so much! You're very kind. Just call if there's a problem."

Tom walked over to Mrs. Pierson on his way out. "I'm not sure you recognize me, Mrs. Pierson. I'm Tom Francis."

"No! From my church? My goodness!"

"Yes. We live next to the church on Mississauga Road. I preach on Sundays and work the hydro lines during the week."

"I am so sorry! My glasses broke when I fell last night. It's good to see you, dear young man."

"And you, too. Well, we're off to work so folks can cook their turkeys." He turned to leave but stopped. "Oh, your farm will be up and running, soon. Goodbye, ma'am. I'm sorry about your fall. You are one of the nicest people I've ever met." He reached out to shake her hand. Immediately, a loud growling sound caused him to recoil.

"Oh, dear! My coyote gets upset when he meets new people." Mrs. Pierson lifted a corner of the quilt to reveal the snarling face of Cody. "But what a lovely thing to say!"

Tom backed up quickly. "A coyote?"

"Not an ordinary coyote, Tom dear," said Mrs. Pierson. "This is Cody. Surely you've heard of him."

Tom's eyes widened as he stared. "I thought he was a local legend."

Bob stepped closer to take a look. "Well, I'll be. He's real."

Cody's growl intensified, and Mrs. Pierson said, "We mustn't push our luck. He's a legend, but he *is* a wild animal. You're a little too close for his comfort."

Both men stepped back at the same time. "Not a problem," said Bob, holding his hands up in submission. They said their goodbyes and departed.

"Merry Christmas!" called Tom as he closed the kitchen door.

"Bye, dears!" Mrs. Pierson called after them. "Merry Christmas!"

Hannah closed the door behind them. "I hope we didn't scare them."

"My goodness. Reverend Tom Francis. He gives beautiful sermons, and he is so generous with his time. Our congregation can't afford a full-time minister." Mrs. Pierson tucked Cody back under the blanket, where he settled contentedly.

With the men gone, Bird said, "Aunt Hannah, I can't believe the gorgeous bridle you and Paul gave me. I love it. It's incredible! Thank you!"

Hannah wiped her hands on her apron and gave Bird a hug. "Merry Christmas, darling. I'm glad you're pleased.

Since you were sleeping, I thought we could do presents in a different way this year." She grinned. "And I knew you'd go outside to see Sunny as soon as you were up."

"Well played!" Normally, they sat around the tree and opened gifts in front of each other. This way was just fine, Bird thought. "I have something for you, too. I hope you like it." She handed a gift bag to her aunt.

Hannah opened the bag. "Oh! Lovely!" She examined two white hand towels embroidered with 'Saddle Creek' in dark green, with a black riding hat and whip. "Bird, these are perfect! I'll put them in the powder room in the hall right now. How thoughtful."

"I got them done in Orangeville. I'm glad you like them."

"I sure do!"

"Mrs. Pierson, I'm sorry. I didn't get you anything for Christmas. I didn't know you'd be here."

"Bird, dear. You saved my life last night. Is there a bigger gift than life?"

Bird found she had a lump in her throat and couldn't say a word. She hugged this little old lady whom she so cherished.

Hannah started working on a cheese platter. She asked Bird to get the best cutlery and the Christmas napkins and plates organized and to set the table in the dining room. "Don't forget the Menorah, Bird."

"I won't. I'll put it on the sideboard like always." It had been a family tradition to pay tribute to their Jewish family and friends celebrating Chanukah for as long as

Bird could remember. "Where is everybody?" she asked, as she began her task.

"Paul went to pick up Grandma Jean, and Eva is lying down before dinner. Guess where Julia is?"

Bird laughed. "Watching *The Muppet Christmas Carol*!"

"Good guess," smiled Hannah. Watching that old film was a tradition for Julia each year, and she hadn't missed it once.

Since he'd entered the room, Stuart hadn't taken part in the conversation and had sat in silence at the round kitchen table. He appeared pensive, with frown lines on his forehead.

Finally, Mrs. Pierson decided to ask. "Tell us what's on your mind, Stuart, dear. How can we help?"

"I'm not sure you can," he answered.

Mrs. Pierson tilted her head and smiled gently. "Give us the chance."

"Okay." Stuart inhaled and chose his words carefully. "Is Christmas always like this for Eva?"

Hannah and Bird stopped moving. "Again?" Hannah asked.

"Let me put it a different way," he said. "Is Eva always like this at Christmas?"

"I'd like to pretend I don't know what you mean, but I do," answered Hannah.

"I definitely know what you mean," nodded Bird.

"I don't." Mrs. Pierson looked from face to face. "Like what?"

Stuart slumped in his chair. "Emotional."

Bird added, "Tempestuous, selfish, childish, mean."

"Bird!" Then Hannah sighed. "Don't forget loud."

"Loud?" asked Mrs. Pierson. "Please tell me what you're talking about."

Hannah answered. "Loud, as in she's always upset about something. It's hard to explain. There's an element of this behaviour at other times, too, but at Christmas it's much more accentuated." She looked at Stuart. "I don't mean to offend you or make you defensive, but you asked. I love Eva."

Stuart clasped his hands together and put his elbows on the table. "I love her, too. I always defend her and stand up for her. But we're family here. I want to know how to help."

"That's really good of you," said Hannah.

"But dumb." Bird felt her insides harden. "No matter what you do, she'll never change. That's just who she is."

Stuart very quietly said, "I keep hoping the best of her will shine. I'm not sure how much more I can take."

"Oh, Stuart, dear," said Mrs. Pierson. "You mustn't say things like that. You must keep trying."

Stuart pursed his lips. "I hear you, Mrs. Pierson. And I do keep trying. But she pushes me away and won't let me help her. You know this, Bird. Some things she says are hard to forgive."

"There's a reason why she's had so many men in her life," said Bird bluntly. "Nobody stays for long."

"Bird!" exclaimed Hannah and Mrs. Pierson together.

Stuart reacted. "No, no. I'm not going to leave her, Bird. It's that I don't know what to do. I need advice. She won't listen when I try to help. She gets mad." He looked down at his clasped hands.

Hannah asked, "What happened this time?"

Stuart paused, and said, "She had a … meltdown at my school's Christmas party."

"And you're the principal," said Bird. "You must have been embarrassed."

"Well, more sad, actually. People don't know what to make of her and tend to judge her badly. She's her own worst enemy."

"What happened at the party?" asked Hannah. "Or do I want to know?"

"Let me guess," answered Bird. "She got drunk and started making passes at all the men in the room?"

Stuart fidgeted. "Now, Bird. It wasn't that bad. She drank a bit more than she should've and began to, er, dance around the room."

"See!" exclaimed Bird. "That's exactly what I said! She'll never change. That's disgusting."

"Bird, dear," Mrs. Pierson reprimanded. "Your mother might have problems but she's still your mother."

Bird stared at her, tears streaming down her face. "You have no idea, do you? If it were only at Christmas, I could get over it. But she gets upset about little things all the time. Or not, which is very confusing. Maybe you don't remember, but she convinced one of her boyfriends that I wasn't her child! She dumped me here like a bag of garbage!"

Hannah came to Bird's side. "Honey, please don't cry. Everybody's on your team, here."

"It sure doesn't seem like it!"

"I'm sorry, dear!" blurted Mrs. Pierson. "I didn't mean to upset you."

Bird wasn't finished. "And you're right, Stuart. It's always way worse at Christmas. She's wrecked every Christmas I can remember. I hate Christmas."

Bird turned to storm out of the room, but was bumped back when the hall door swung open, heralding the sudden entrance of Eva. She stood at the door frame in a model's pose, with her head tilted, chin up, one knee bent in front of the other and one shoulder back.

Silence. Each of them wondered how much Eva had heard, and they waited for the temper tantrum.

Instead, Eva smiled gaily and plopped herself on Stuart's lap. She rearranged her sassy red satin dress and crossed one leg over the other, showing her red lace slip. Her tall heels were scarlet red, and her shiny lipstick was the same shade. She cooed, "I had a wonderful nap and dressed for dinner. I'm all refreshed."

"Good, good!" said Stuart, astonished. "You look wonderful."

"Wonderful!" gushed Hannah.

"How lovely, dear," chimed in Mrs. Pierson.

Bird glared at each person, one by one. "You're all afraid of her, aren't you. I'm going upstairs to shower."

"About time!" chortled Eva. "You stink like the barn, and your hair is filthy. Scrub yourself, Bird, or nobody will sit beside you at dinner." She thought she was quite amusing, and she threw back her head and laughed. Then, in a confidential tone, she added, "I can't do anything with that girl!"

Bird looked directly at Mrs. Pierson. "Are you beginning to get the picture?" With that, she turned and left the room.

She went directly upstairs and closed her door. There had never been a good Christmas to date, and this was just like all the rest. Why was this one, solitary day in every year set up to be such a big deal? she wondered. Who was happy at Christmas, anyway? Perfect people with perfect families? Did they even exist? The entire concept of Christmas was designed to point out any imperfection in your life. Bah, humbug.

Paul's truck came to a stop at the front door. From her upstairs window, Bird watched her grandmother get out of the truck with Paul's assistance. George, Grandma Jean's second husband, couldn't come. His daughter from his first marriage was celebrating Christmas with him. George's daughter did not get along with Jean — at all — so this was a good solution.

Grandma Jean was Hannah and Eva's mother, and Bird could vaguely see the family resemblance. Her pale blond hair was stiff with spray, and her black mink was draped elegantly around her slim build. Her feet were encased in soft leather boots, and under her arm she held her black clutch purse and leather shoe bag. Grandma Jean had style, Bird noted. Too bad she never had fun.

Her Grandma Jean held very high standards of etiquette for everybody around her, but the standards she held for herself were the highest of all. Bird had never heard her burp, let alone "pass wind." Bird mouthed, "fart."

Paul gallantly led Jean through the front door. Bird heard him shout, "Grandma Jean's here!" followed by the whump of the big, old door closing behind them.

Just then Julia peeked her head around the door frame of Bird's room. "Hey. Going down?"

"I'll be a few minutes," Bird answered. "I need a shower."

"I've got something for you." Julia giggled as she handed Bird a long, narrow box wrapped in Christmas paper. "I really hope you like it."

"And I've got something for you, too." Bird smiled and dug a small, brightly coloured bag out of her backpack.

"Let's open them together," suggested Julia. "This is so exciting!"

Bird tore open the package to find a belt with tiny silver horseshoes and bits glued to it. "Awesome, Julia! I love it!"

At the same time, Julia held up the pair of long, thin socks covered in pictures of horses that Bird had given her, to be worn under riding boots. "Thanks, Bird! I'll be so cool!"

The girls gave each other a happy hug.

"Merry Christmas," said Bird, then pushed her away to take a better look at her sister. "What the heck are you wearing, Julia?"

Julia turned slowly around to show Bird her outfit. "It's my Christmas present. Mom made me promise to wear it. Is it horrible?"

"Yes." Bird's eyes took in the slinky red polyester jumpsuit with floppy frills on the plunging neckline. Julia's earrings were large white Christmas bells with red holly berries, with matching barrettes, which wouldn't stay put in her straight, thin hair. On her feet she wore red ballet slippers, and a red furry boa scarf was wrapped around her neck. Tufts of red fluff floated down every time she moved.

"Yes," Bird repeated. "Horrible. And groom your boa."

"It's vintage. I think I'm allergic. What did she give you?"

"Nothing. And looking at you, I'm glad."

"Should I change? The truth, Bird?"

"The truth is, it doesn't matter. It's only family."

"But, should I be a rebel and wear something else?"

"Are you comfortable in that?"

"Totally — if I don't look in the mirror."

Bird and Julia laughed, then said in unison, "Then don't look in the mirror!" as Julia flounced out the door.

Once Bird had had her shower, she felt a lot better. She hated to admit it, but her mother had been right about her filth. In her defence, she'd been up all night rescuing Mrs. Pierson and Cody in the storm. She'd earned her grime.

Bird vowed to keep her cool at dinner for Hannah's sake. Her aunt had worked hard to make this dinner a success. Even if Eva made her crazy, she would behave herself.

Still, it was tempting to have a little fun at Eva's expense. Bird looked through her wardrobe and cast her eyes around the room. The red sheets on her bed jumped out at her, and she made a decision. If red was the colour of the day, so be it. At least it wasn't pink.

Bird was ready. She silently entered the living room and waited to be noticed. The party was in full force. Jean was complacently nursing her second martini. Stuart and Paul were pouring wine for the guests and passing bowls of cashews. Cliff was sitting with Mrs. Pierson, chatting about the old days and memories of Pete. Hannah was bringing in condiments and readying the table for dinner. Eva was fixing Julia's hair because the barrettes kept sliding out.

"I'm fine without them, Mom," said Julia patiently.

"The outfit needs them. They're the finishing touch."

Julia was the first to see Bird. "Holy moly!"

Bird struck the same pose that Eva had done earlier, with her chin up, her legs bent and one shoulder back. It was trickier than she expected, and she had a bit of trouble balancing on the sparkly gold heels she'd found in her mother's room.

Bird had fashioned the red sheet from her bed into a toga, with her left shoulder bare, and clinched it at the waist with Julia's Christmas belt. She'd pinned the red pillowcase into a turban and dragged a red bath towel behind her like a fur coat in an old movie. The finishing touch, aside from Eva's excessively high heels, was a red chiffon scarf that she'd found at the bottom of Eva's suitcase, which she'd tied in an enormous bow beneath her chin.

"Bird, you look ridiculous! Get upstairs this minute!" gasped Eva. "Oh, my good gold *shoes*! Get them off now! I said NOW!" She was red in the face and bellowing. "You'll *ruin* them!"

Bird ignored her as she did the model strut into the middle of the room and turned to show all sides of her ensemble.

Stuart went to calm Eva, but she threw off his attempt. "Get away from me!"

Jean stood up unsteadily. "Eva. Keep your voice down. You sound like a fishwife. Where's the ladies' room?"

Cliff began to chuckle until Hannah shushed him. "This is not funny, Cliff. Dinner is ready, and now we've got trouble."

"Trouble?" exclaimed Mrs. Pierson. "My dear, there's no amount of trouble that can't be solved with a nice chiffon scarf." She squinted at Bird, unsure of what she was seeing. "That is chiffon, isn't it, dear? How glamorous."

"Oh my gawd! That's my good chiffon scarf!" Eva lunged at Bird with intent, but was accidentally blocked by Grandma Jean as she stumbled to the washroom. The two women fell to the ground, shrieking with the shock.

Eva got back up quickly. Her dress had slipped off her shoulders to reveal lacy undergarments. She angrily straightened her scarlet dress and puffed her hair back into place.

Bird's eyes grew huge, and she covered her mouth with her hands. This was way more exciting than she could have hoped for.

Cliff howled with laughter, unable to contain it any longer. "This is hilarious! Is it a Christmas tradition, like a pantomime?"

Hannah stepped into the room nervously. Paul noticed her distress and rushed to her side. He took her arm. "It's a joke, Hannah. Bird wanted to get Eva's goat, and she succeeded."

"Should I put dinner on the table?" she asked him. "The potatoes will get cold."

Jean was having trouble getting to her feet and reached out to Eva. "Help me up," she demanded.

"Clumsy cow," Eva muttered, refusing to help her mother.

"W-what did you call me?" Jean stuttered in disbelief.

"You knocked me over!" Eva snapped back.

"Not on purpose, you little tramp," Jean retorted bitterly. "Someone! Give me a hand!"

"You called me a tramp? Really?"

"You called me a cow!"

"You're jealous, admit it!" Eva yelled. She pointed her finger at Jean as she struggled on the floor. "You've always been jealous! I was Daddy's favourite girl, not you!"

The oddness of that remark silenced the room.

Bird slowly untied the chiffon scarf and slipped off the shoes. She had not intended to ruin the party.

Eva looked like she'd seen a ghost.

Hannah spoke up. In the stillness, she asked, "What are you saying, Eva?"

"I don't know. I don't know, Hannah. Except that … except I think it's true."

Stuart approached Eva, but didn't touch her. "Honey, let's sit down. You need to take a minute."

Eva nodded and let Stuart guide her to the settee, where she plunked down limply. Stuart sat beside her. Eva put her head on his shoulder.

Paul helped Grandma Jean to her feet. She was rattled. He walked slowly with her to the washroom.

Cliff whispered, "Hannah? I'm sorry. I thought it was a thing, a Christmas thing, or something." Because nobody else was making a sound, his voice sounded loud.

"Don't worry, Cliff. We're all at sea. But we can't let it ruin Christmas." Hannah straightened her shoulders and spoke loudly. "Okay! Dinner is served! Come to the table. Julia wrote out lovely name cards, so please find your seats."

Everybody stood up and obediently headed to the dining room. Nobody spoke.

In the confusion, Bird dashed upstairs. She fell on her bed. What was that all about? she wondered.

Something close to honesty was at hand, and Bird's nose for truth was twitching.

5 REVELATION

Deck the halls with boughs of holly,
Fa la la la la, la la la la ...

By the time Bird reappeared in her sweater and jeans, all the guests were seated at the table. She slipped into the only vacancy, in the chair between Stuart and Jean.

Hannah had pasted her "company" smile on to her face as she placed bowls of steaming vegetables on the table. Julia was busy helping her, while Paul carved the turkey.

"Who likes dark and who likes white?" he asked heartily.

Jean raised her wine glass. "Red or white, I don't care! Who's pouring?"

Bird watched her grandmother with interest. Jean drank heavily, but not usually when there were witnesses. Normally, she would behave herself impeccably, then go home to get wasted.

Stuart dutifully filled her glass.

"I like dark meat, thanks," answered Bird. "But first, may I please apologize?"

All eyes turned to her.

"I only meant to have a laugh, when I got all dressed up in red like Mom and Julia, I mean. And what I didn't mean was for anybody's feelings to be hurt or for anybody to fall down."

Eva took a breath as if to speak. Bird looked at her expectantly. Then Eva shook her head and cast her eyes down.

Stuart spoke softly, with a kind smile. "Thank you, Bird. Your apology is accepted." He patted Eva's hand. "By all of us. It takes a big person to say they're sorry."

"I thought you looked lovely, dear," added Mrs. Pierson.

Cliff shrugged and said, "I still have no idea what happened, Bird, but I thought you were funny."

"Me, too!" agreed Julia. Her grin disappeared when she saw that everyone else looked serious.

Hannah trilled, "Here's the gravy, and I'm sitting down! Julia, you, too! Now, let's hold hands and say grace."

Suddenly, the lights went out. The room was thrown into complete darkness. A collective sigh was released, almost like it was all right to relax, and nobody needed to pretend that things were normal as long as it was dark. Like a play at the theatre, Bird thought. And they were all actors.

There was a knock on the door. Lucky began to bark.

Hannah lit one candle, paused, and when nobody moved said, "Bird, can you get the door, please?"

"Sure." She jumped up and ran to the front hall. When she opened the door, there was no one there. Lucky stopped barking.

He ran outside with his tail wagging. *Good person, good person!*

Who is it, Lucky?

Friend not foe! Friend not foe!

"Hello?" Bird called.

Cody slipped out the door like a shadow under Bird's feet.

Cody? Where are you going?

Out. There is a strange and unknowable energy in the house.

True. But are you feeling well enough?

Much better. Call on me if there is danger.

I will. And come back if you want.

The small coyote disappeared into the night as Bird stepped out on the porch and looked around. "Hello? Who's there?"

Suddenly, she was enveloped in Alec's arms. He hugged her tightly and murmured in her ear, "I'm glad it was you who answered the door."

"Did you plan on grabbing whoever answered?" she teased.

"Yes. Especially your Grandma Jean."

"She would've called the police."

"Exactly."

"Alec, we were going to talk about being just friends, remember?"

"You said that, not me. I don't agree one bit."

"But it's weird, now. Isn't it?"

"No! And why? My father and your aunt can get married if they choose. We're not even remotely related."

"You're right, but ..."

"Do *you* think it's weird, Bird?"

"No. But other people might."

"When did you ever worry about what other people think? I've never heard you say that before!"

"Let's talk later. Let go of me before I start kissing you."

Alec kissed her right on the lips. Briefly, Bird resisted feebly, then gave in to the overwhelming attraction.

Hannah called from the dining room. "Bird? Who's there?"

They jerked apart, giggling quietly. Bird called, "It's Alec! Here for Christmas dinner." She looked at him. "Aren't you supposed to be with your mother?"

"I was. We had Christmas lunch. The dishes are done so I came over." He smiled warmly at her. "Do you mind?"

"You know I don't. It's amazing to have you here. Christmas might be saved yet."

"That bad?"

"You have no idea."

When they walked into the room, Bird was pleased to see how festive the room looked with the candles cheerfully twinkling on the table, and the lit Menorah on the sideboard.

Paul put down the carving knife and embraced his son. "Alec! What a wonderful surprise. Please, grab a seat!"

Hannah scurried in with a chair from the kitchen. "I'll put you between Julia and me, Alec. How are the roads?"

"Safe, if you take it slow," he answered. "The fog is clearing, and most of the traffic lights are back on. I see you still don't have hydro."

Julia said, "We had electricity until a minute ago, but it's so romantic to have candles, and the food is cooked so we don't really care, at least until the house gets cold and then we might not like it." The girl's chatter died down and then she smiled. "I'm glad you're here, Alec."

"Hey, Julia," he said. "Me, too."

Jean peered at Alec. "Who is this boy?"

"My son, Alec," answered Paul. "I thought you'd met him before. Excuse me for not introducing you. Mrs. Bradley, please meet Alec Daniels."

"Hello, Mrs. Bradley," said Alec with a smile. "We've met a few times, but always with a lot of people."

"Perhaps," Jean sniffed. "Perhaps not."

"And you know everybody else, I think, Alec?" asked Paul.

Alec looked around the table. "I sure do. Hello, Mrs. Pierson! Good to see you."

Mrs. Pierson took his hand, and her eyes twinkled at him. "You are a dear, dear boy."

"And Julia, of course. And Mr. and Mrs. Gilmour, hello."

Stuart said, "Welcome!" Eva smiled slightly and nodded.

Cliff stood up. "Alec, buddy! Good to see you."

"Hey, Cliff! What's happening?"

"Well, actually, I just got a text from my son. He's on his way with the whole family, and they're bringing dinner. I better get home to tidy up. My place is a mess!"

Hannah raised her hands. "Bring them over, Cliff! There's lots to eat! We'd love to have them. The more, the merrier!"

Bird saw her aunt's desperation, and she felt badly that she'd started this whole thing with the red sheets. The party was falling apart.

Cliff nodded a few times awkwardly before saying, "I think tonight it's better we have our own little Christmas. But I appreciate the offer. Thanks."

Bird walked Cliff to the door. She whispered, "I don't blame you. Are they really coming?"

"They're really coming. Highway 400 is open down to Highway 9, and Highway 10 is clear."

"Can I do night check? Please? I need an excuse to get out of here later."

He snorted. "Understood. That'd be good. Two flakes for all of them, except the ponies — one small flake only — and three for Sunny. He's still tired from your rescue mission."

"Okay. I'll give them a little Christmas treat. I made them."

"Sure. But not Josh. He'll choke. And Simon can't have sugar."

"I know. It's not sugar, and I'll make a treat soup for Josh."

"A small one. He's on a special diet."

"Got it."

Cliff stepped outside. "If things get too crazy here, just call me. I can do night check, no problem."

"Too crazy is exactly why I need to do it."

Bird went back to the dining room and sat down. Alec was across the table from her. He winked, and she winked back.

Jean noticed, and asked, "So who are you again, young man?"

"I'm Paul's son," he enunciated slowly and clearly.

"I'm not deaf. Why did you wink at Alberta?"

Julia jumped in. "Because he has a crush on her!"

"You're Paul's son? Tsk tsk. You're almost family, boy. That's not on." Jean took another drink of wine. She repeated the two words forcefully. "Not … on." She shook her head and pursed her lips.

Alec looked shocked. His mouth opened but no words came out. He looked at Bird, who raised her eyebrows sympathetically and shrugged slightly. Grandma Jean had made her point for her, but this was no time to be proven right, Bird thought.

Silence descended on the table like an Arctic chill.

Eva hadn't said a word since she and her mother had collided earlier. Now she leaned forward. "Mother, that was odd, coming from you."

Jean's head shot up, and her eyes focused on her younger daughter. "What on *earth* do you mean?"

"You are very quick to judge family relationships."

Her voice had dropped to a small whisper. "What about ours?"

Jean looked at Eva sideways. "What are you talking about?"

"Do you remember when I was a child?"

"Of course I do." Jean's response was dismissive, and with a quick roll of her eyes she indicated that it was a foolish question.

Eva's face contorted. The flickering candlelight gave her an otherworldly appearance. "Do you remember how Daddy tickled me and wouldn't stop? And how he wanted me to have naps with him?"

Bird snapped to attention. Tickling? Naps?

Jean's tone changed to slightly aggressive. "Yes. He was an affectionate father. At least to you." Her precise diction inferred that the conversation was finished.

Eva wasn't put off. "I remember you called me that name — 'a little tramp' — when I was a small girl. I remember that. I remember things that happened a long time ago."

"What are you babbling about, Eva?" Jean was now on the defensive. She raised her voice. "You lived in a dream world with your Barbie dolls, Eva. Play acting. Making things up. *Silly* things."

"Was I, Mom? Making things up?" Eva breathed deeply. When she exhaled, her breath was ragged. "Is that why you never believed me?"

"You loved playing with your father!" Jean exclaimed with indignation. "You ran to him to be cuddled. And all that 'sugar pie' stuff! It made me gag."

Nobody spoke. Bird realized that she'd stopped breathing. Many times she'd heard her grandfather call Eva 'sugar pie,' and Hannah 'lemon pie.' She looked at Aunt Hannah's stricken face. She appeared to be frozen.

"And what has this got to do with that boy?" demanded Jean, pointing at Alec. "You changed the subject entirely. He should not be dating Bird. It's almost incest!"

"Really?" Eva whispered. Her volume was low, but Bird felt her electric intensity. "Do you remember when I was about five, Mom? Hannah was maybe seven. Daddy came home from the company Christmas party and wanted me to take a nap with him. Do you remember?"

"Eva, surely you don't expect me to remember every detail of your childhood." Jean impatiently drained her glass. She nudged Stuart, who added an inch of wine.

"No, I don't. And I don't remember every detail, either," said Eva. "But I remember this like it was yesterday. He told me that his best Christmas present ever was for me to have a nap with him."

Jean was ignoring her. She motioned Stuart to keep pouring. Stuart pretended not to notice.

"Are you listening, Mom?"

"No. I'm busy being properly attended." Jean seized the bottle from Stuart and poured until her glass was full to the brim.

Eva watched her mother set the empty bottle down with a thud and then said, "I need your attention, Mom. Now."

Nobody moved a muscle. Bird noticed how her Grandma Jean's mouth clamped shut and her lips pressed together.

Eva continued. "He came home reeking of alcohol. I hated that smell."

Jean made a harrumphing noise. "Well, not any longer!"

Nobody laughed at her joke. Eva continued. "Hannah and I were having supper in the kitchen. Macaroni and cheese with ketchup."

With agitation, Jean asked, "Is this the proper place, Eva?" Her voice had become shrill.

Eva trembled visibly and softly cleared her throat.

Bird was mesmerized by the anguish on her mother's face in the light of the candles. Her stomach knotted. She didn't want to hear what her mother was about to say. Bird wanted to run but found she'd lost the use of her limbs.

Eva answered hoarsely. "I don't know, Mom. What is the proper place? Not when I was little. I tried. As far as I know, there *is* no proper place to ask your mother if she knew her husband was abusing their child."

Jean fell off her chair sideways, onto the floor. It happened so quickly that nobody could react in time to catch her.

The overhead lights fluttered and then shone brightly, blinding everyone. Their eyes had become adjusted to the dim candlelight, and it took a moment for people to get their bearings.

Paul was the closest to Jean, and he knelt to check her air passage, to be sure it was clear, then reached for a glass of water. He splashed a little water on her face, and held the glass to her lips. She took a sip.

"She'll be fine, folks," he said. He pulled the seat cushion off his chair and tucked it under Jean's head as she lay on the floor.

Bird still couldn't move. It was as if her body had no muscle and was made of stone. She had sensed her mother's pain all her life, and she had always known that something was drastically amiss between her mother and her grandfather. But why, Bird wondered, had she never put the two together?

Maybe she never wanted to believe it. She would examine this more closely when she was able to think. Right now, her mind was on autopilot as she recollected her mother's baby voice when men were around, the girlish clothes with bows and frills, and how Eva demanded male attention in every possible way.

Hannah plopped into her chair, bringing Bird out of her thoughts. She observed the emotions as they crossed her aunt's face. Shock, concern, disbelief, then acceptance.

"Oh my God, Eva." Hannah spoke slowly and quietly. "I didn't know *what* was wrong, but I knew *something* was wrong."

"I didn't understand myself." Eva looked sadly at her sister. "I still don't, really."

Stuart held Eva's hand in support, and he leaned across the corner of the table to place his other hand on Hannah's.

Laura Pierson, with her ankle raised on a stool, spoke clearly. "It might not seem so now, but this is very good. Truth will set you free." She spoke with conviction and intensity. "Listen, everyone. Listen to an old woman. Truth must be handled with love, and most especially, kindness. If not, everything that you've ever had as a family will corrode and be destroyed. I've seen it happen."

Mrs. Pierson's stark warning reverberated around the room. Bird tried to process the wisdom. She repeated it in her head. *Truth must be handled with love and kindness or it will destroy everything.* She needed to write it down before she forgot.

The dinner sat untouched. The festive china and the good cutlery and the seasonal serving dishes and Hannah's finest tablecloth and napkins mocked them. The Santa and Mrs. Claus salt and pepper shakers looked almost sinister in the glaring light of this revelation.

Paul helped Jean back into her chair. To Bird, it seemed like her grandmother had aged ten years, and she'd looked quite old before.

Jean licked her dry lips. "Eva. I never saw anything untoward." Her face was pale. Her right hand had a tremor.

"Did … you know?" Eva's eyes beseeched her mother. Bird was sure that Eva needed to hear the truth.

Jean paused. "I didn't *want* to know."

Bingo, Bird thought. The simple truth.

Eva sat back. Her head dropped and muffled sobs emanated from deep in her throat.

"Wait. Eva." Jean tried to rise from her chair but sat back down. "I didn't mean it like it came out." Her face shook and her hands raised, palms up. "I meant that I didn't want anything like that to be happening. If anything like that *had* been going on, I would not have tolerated it." Jean looked around the table for support. She almost pleaded, "I couldn't accuse him without proof, now, could I?"

Eva looked up. Her eyes glistened with tears and even forgiveness, Bird thought. She whispered, "No. You couldn't. Thank you, Mom," and made a feeble attempt at a smile.

So much pain filled the room that again Bird yearned to flee. She thought of Cody's words as he slipped out the front door. *There is a strange and unknowable energy in the house.* She willed herself to stay and wondered how she could help.

Grandma Jean could hardly breathe, and Eva looked destroyed. Bird had the sense that a hug might do wonders right now. But Eva never hugged Bird, and Jean never hugged at all. So she quietly leaned over to her grandmother and kissed her cheek. Jean sniffed and turned her head away, but then relented. "Thank you, Bird," she whispered.

Bird then stood and moved to Eva's side. "Mom, I love you."

Eva's eyes overflowed. She croaked, "I love you, too." Rarely had Bird heard those words from her mother. And they sounded true.

"I've caused a scene. I need to go home," Jean mumbled meekly. She stood up and stumbled, then caught herself and stood straight with her shoulders back. Now she spoke loudly, with her usual command. "Paul? Do you mind?"

"Not at all!" he said. "Hannah? Can you get your mother's coat and bag? I'll heat up the truck and bring it to the front."

"Of course," answered Hannah. "Please, everyone, please help yourself. Everything's cold, nothing is as planned, but you should not go hungry." She rushed to organize her mother's departure, glad, Bird thought, to have something positive to do.

Stuart took Eva's elbow and helped her stand. Together, they retired to a quiet spot in the living room to have some time alone.

The only one left at the table was Mrs. Pierson, sitting quietly with her swollen foot still up on the stool. Bird sat beside her. Alec sat down, too, and took Bird's hand in his. Julia joined them after changing into her jeans and a lively Christmas sweater covered in snowmen.

"Well, now. It's just the very old and the very young," said Mrs. Pierson. "Let's hold hands and each say what we're most thankful for. You start, Julia."

Julia thought for a second. "I'm thankful for my sister, Bird. Especially now. If I didn't have you, Bird, I'd feel even more confused and so alone." Julia's smile was lopsided and uncertain.

"I'm grateful for you, Julia," said Bird. "I don't understand what Mom's story is yet. I mean, what happened and everything, and I don't know what's next. I only know I'm happy to be facing this with you, my little sister. And, I'm grateful for Alec, for Mrs. Pierson, for Aunt Hannah, Paul, Stuart, and Mom. And for Cody, Sunny, and Lucky."

Under the table, Lucky's tail began to thump. *Good dog, good dog!* He messaged.

Bird smiled. *Yes, Lucky, you're a good dog.*

Alec asked, "Is it my turn?"

"Yes, dear boy," said Mrs. Pierson. "Go ahead."

"I'm grateful for Bird." His eyes shone as he looked at her, and Bird felt a thrill down to her toes. "And that I'm here tonight. I didn't expect such a dramatic Christmas dinner, but I'm honoured to be a part of this family, for better and for worse."

"Now it's my turn." Mrs. Pierson squeezed Bird's hand. "I'm thankful for so much, but tonight I have four things to say." Her head shook slightly as she got her thoughts in order. She smiled sadly. "At Christmas I think of my darling Pete. We had so many wonderful years. That's one." Mrs. Pierson wiped away a small tear that had escaped down her cheek. "I'm thankful that my sons listened to me to cancel their plans when the ice storm came through. I could never forgive myself if they'd been in an accident trying to be with me." She paused. "That's two. The third one is that I'm thankful that Bird and Sunny and Cody rescued me. I would not be alive if they had not come when they did." She gave Bird's hand an extra squeeze. "The last one is, I'm grateful that Eva talked openly about those memories now, with people she trusts, so she can begin to heal. She must take the time she needs, no more and no less."

Bird listened. "Why are you so wise, Mrs. Pierson?"

Mrs. Pierson lifted her shoulders slightly and tilted her head. "Age, dear. One learns a lot by living a long time and observing things. But experience, too. Every family has darkness. It's in our nature. We're animals, all of us. Some are more civilized than others."

Bird thought about Kenneth Bradley, who had abused his own daughter. Bird had learned about this in Health class, and she wondered what inappropriate things he'd done to her mother. She shuddered and felt a little queasy.

At any rate, Kenneth Bradley was having Christmas in jail, and that was exactly where he should be. He thought that rules were for other people, not for him. He had no respect for anyone or anything, except his own gratification.

"My grandfather is the darkness in our family," Bird stated. "He is fully *un*civilized."

"Before you jump to that conclusion, dear, and I thoroughly understand why you might," said Mrs. Pierson, "consider what made him the way he is. What horrid events in his life shaped him?"

"Misshaped, more like it," corrected Bird. "And I get what you're saying. But he damaged everyone around him, and now we hear this new thing about Mom, his own little girl!"

Julia said, "Poor Mom. She must be weirded out."

Alec and Bird slowly nodded agreement. Alec said, "She's been through more than I ever guessed. Much more."

"Yes," Mrs. Pierson agreed. "You children will be very important in Eva's healing. And, don't forget that your Grandma Jean needs to heal, too, dears."

Bird knew she was right. Grandma Jean, with her need to be perfect and her emotional distance, would have a very hard time with this. Alec and Julia looked at the old woman quizzically.

Mrs. Pierson spoke so quietly that they had to lean closer to hear. "When Eva was a girl, things were different. People never talked openly about abuse. Back then, it was more common to ignore it and hope it went away."

The three young people nodded as one and listened closely.

Mrs. Pierson inhaled. "My guess is that even if Grandma Jean had suspected something, she didn't know for sure and couldn't confront him. Even when little Eva told her." Mrs. Pierson tapped the table once, with energy. "But, your Grandma Jean was damaged by Kenneth Bradley, too. And, no matter what happened back then, she will be filled with guilt." She sat back. "Thank goodness, now kids learn about such things and are taught what's right and what's not right. And now you can go to a teacher or the police if nobody at home believes you, or it's not safe."

Bird thought about her Health class again, and she knew what Mrs. Pierson said was true. But still, it would be hard to talk about it, she thought, if it were happening to you, especially if it were a parent or a relative.

"Listen, children." Mrs. Pierson wasn't finished. "Your family is not the only family where things like this have happened. I've seen it many times. Families can look totally perfect on the outside and have this secret on the inside. And it's never the child's fault. Children want attention. They crave it, and they trust adults to do right by them. But bad attention doesn't equal love. Bad attention is poisonous. Eva was abused. Eva was hurt."

Mrs. Pierson's words resonated with Bird. Eva was so full of hurt that it just seeped out. Now, so much about her behaviour made more sense. Bird had long wondered why her mother always found Christmas so difficult, and why she consistently did so many hurtful, destructive things. Now she knew.

"But why *tonight*?" asked Julia. "How could Mom *not* talk about something so important for so *long*? It doesn't make sense."

Mrs. Pierson patted Julia's hand. "Sometimes it happens, dear, especially with children, when they can't cope with the betrayal of abuse. Their brains build an imaginary box to put bad things in, a place where the bad things can stay until the time comes to take them out and examine them."

Julia screwed up her face questioningly. "And that time was today?"

"Yes, it was, for whatever reason. Maybe, with people she loves around her, it became safe to talk about it." Mrs. Pierson smiled kindly. "Or maybe it just couldn't wait any longer. It's hard to understand, dear, I know." Mrs. Pierson brightened. She smiled. "It's quite amazing, isn't it, how our brains look after us?"

Bird nodded and said, "Maybe, now that it's out in the open, she'll be more at peace with herself and less unhappy."

"Let's hope so, dear," answered Mrs. Pierson.

"And stop driving us bat-poop crazy?" asked Julia.

Bird gasped and covered her mouth, knowing that she shouldn't find anything funny at this sombre time. Julia suppressed a giggle, and Bird began to chuckle. She picked up someone's discarded wine glass and raised it. "Cheers to that!"

Mrs. Pierson raised her water glass. "Good for you girls! Find the light!"

Alec and Julia grabbed whatever glass was closest at hand. Alec said, "To your mother's happiness!"

Julia added, "Which is our happiness, as well! Happy mama, happy fama-lee!"

Bird felt hopeful, and suddenly very hungry. There would be much more time to think about this, but now she needed a break from the heaviness. She heaped her plate with turkey, mashed potatoes, green beans, and turnip, and covered it all with gravy.

Julia and Alec did the same, and they made a big plate of food for Mrs. Pierson. They began to eat.

Hannah came in and sat at the table with them. After helping Grandma Jean to the truck, she'd checked in with Eva. "Stuart and Eva have gone upstairs. It's been a tough night."

Bird nodded. "Very tough. When will Paul be back?"

"Soon. It's good that Jean and George's place is so close." She smiled warmly. "How did I get so lucky as to have a man like Paul in my life?"

"So why don't you marry him?" asked Julia directly.

Hannah laughed. "I would like nothing more. And he would, too. We keep talking about doing it. It's just a matter of our schedules."

"Can I be a bridesmaid when you do? If I'm not too old by then?"

Hannah chortled. "Sure you can, and Bird, too. That'd make me very happy. And your mother, Eva, will be my matron of honour." She wiped a tear away and said softly, "My little sister. I never knew what she went through. I guess I was too busy trying to survive, myself." She shook her head slightly as she reflected. "Eva was our father's favourite. I always thought he just liked her a whole lot more than me."

"Aunt Hannah, do you think it's true?" Bird asked.

"Eva believes it. And I believe her. Something unhealthy was happening, that's all I know."

Bird and Julia looked at each other, and they knew they had the same question. Julia put it in words. "What do you think happened, exactly?"

Hannah shook her head and said, "I really don't know."

Mrs. Pierson said, "The details don't matter, dears. Eva was damaged. She must be respected. She might share the details one day, or she might decide they're too personal."

She continued, "Understand something, dears. These memories come with feelings of shame and humiliation, even guilt, although it's utterly unfair. Your mother was just a child, but she'll remember being complicit."

Bird tried to understand. "Because she thought his attention equaled love? I get that."

"Yes." Mrs. Pierson squeezed her hand. "It would've seemed like a closeness that she and her father shared."

Hannah nodded. "The house had a weird atmosphere at the best of times. Complicated. We never knew what was safe and what wasn't."

"Do you have any memories like that?" Bird asked.

"No. But that doesn't negate Eva's memories."

Mrs. Pierson poured more congealed gravy on to her turkey. "Listen to your aunt, children. Do not question your mother's memories. The whole story might eventually be told. We must be patient." She took a forkful of mashed potatoes, but stopped before it got to her mouth. "Aren't you eating, dear Hannah?"

"I'll wait for Paul. You go ahead."

Nobody minded that the food was cold.

6 NIGHT CHECK

Silent night, holy night,
All is calm, all is bright …

It was time to do night check. Bird and Alec walked together out to the barn, holding hands. Bird carried her bag of Christmas horse treats in the other.

They would fill the water buckets and give the horses their hay to munch on during the night. It was an essential evening duty. Very rarely would they find a problem, but if a horse had colic, which was a terrible stomach ache, or had become cast in the stall, which meant that he was stuck and couldn't get up, immediate action must be taken. Or if a horse hadn't finished his dinner, or hadn't drunk any water, they'd make a plan to take turns watching him. When all the horses were acting normally, their human custodians could sleep soundly at night.

Cody followed them. Bird thought he looked better than the night before, but he was still stiff and weak.

Bird girl. There's a special present for you in the barn.

Really? From you, Cody?

No. Not this time. You'll see. The coyote disappeared again, into the darkness. *My present to you will come later.*

I don't need a present, Bird messaged. But he was gone.

"Your poor mother," said Alec. "She was very brave to do what she did tonight. I have a new respect for her."

"So do I. It took me totally by surprise. I hope you don't mind."

"What? Why would I mind?"

"I don't know. To be put in the middle of the strangest thing that's ever happened in my very strange family? Or maybe I wonder if you mind that I *have* such a strange family."

Alec stopped walking. He turned Bird to face him and said, "I felt privileged to be included." He touched her cheek. "I'll always be there for you, you know."

"I know. But I have … problems with her, problems that I'm not sure I can get past. She's been really tough on me. You know that." Bird looked at him earnestly. "I couldn't say it in there when everybody was so compassionate and caring, but even though I know I should, I'm not sure I'll be able to get past all her crazy crap. I want to, Alec, but I'm not as nice as you think I am."

Alec smiled. "Yes you are. You're very nice."

"I'm not really. Can I suddenly trust her not to ridicule me? Can I let my defences down and risk getting slammed?" Bird wiped her cheek and nose with her sleeve.

"Not in one day! It's totally understandable after what she's put you through. One day at a time, Bird. You can start just by talking to her."

Bird shook her head. "That's the problem, Alec. My mother and I don't do that. We never talk!" Now her tears flowed. "We never did!"

Alec pulled her into his embrace and waited until Bird's shoulders relaxed and her sobbing ebbed. He whispered, "You can do this, Bird. I'll help in whatever way I can."

Bird sniffed back her emotion. "Thank you."

"Anyway, Christmas lunch at my house was boring."

She barked out a laugh. "Boring is good."

Alec took her hand again, and they continued up to the barn. "Look at the sky, Bird." Alec gazed upward, and Bird did the same. "It's a beautiful night."

"Crazy how horrible it was last night in the ice storm, and now it's like this. Calm and almost balmy in twenty-four hours."

"Almost like Mother Nature apologizing."

"Poetic, as well as handsome? Too good to be true." Bird smiled happily as she opened the barn door and flicked on the lights. She stopped. "Strange," she murmured.

"Why?"

"They always nicker and make a fuss when I come in. Not because they like me, but because they want their evening hay."

Bird, you have company.

Company? Who's here, Sunny?

One clue. The man who talks like you.

Fred? My father's here?

He's in the tack room. He gave us our hay and filled our water to the top.

"Okay, Alec," said Bird. "Eva's revelation wasn't enough for this day. There's another surprise for you. Are you ready?"

"Ah. Not sure. Why are you being so odd?"

"I'm not being odd."

"So why're you creeping down the barn aisle like that?"

She stopped her beeline to the tack room and straightened up, unaware of the effect this news had on her until Alec mentioned it.

"My father's here," she whispered.

"Where?"

"In the tack room."

"How do you know that?"

"Sunny told me."

"Yeah."

"Take a look." She threw open the tack room door. Fred Sweetree sat in the chair beside the saddle rack, looking very comfortable.

He smiled his beautiful smile. His dark eyes shone brightly with quiet strength. "Hello, Alberta. Merry Christmas."

"Fred. Dad. Merry Christmas!" Bird ran into his arms and hugged this person who had been a mystery to her all her life, and she expected always would be. "I'm so glad you're here. I can't believe it."

"I'm passing through. I felt you might need me tonight."

Bird nodded slowly. Her father's skills were much more highly developed than her own, she thought. "Thank you."

Fred cast his gaze at Alec. "Hello. I'm Bird's father."

Alec was still amazed that Bird knew he'd be sitting there before they opened the door. "Yes, I guessed that's who you are. I mean Bird told me that Sunny told her. Anyway, I'm Alec Daniels, Paul's son."

"And Bird's boyfriend."

Alec and Bird looked at each other. Bird said, "No point in dancing around it. My father reads people's minds. Not just animals'."

Alec grinned. He put out his hand for Fred to shake. "Yes. I'm Bird's boyfriend, if she'll have me."

Fred's grin matched Alec's. "Good for you."

"Dad, why are you here, really?"

"To wish you a Merry Christmas."

Bird tilted her head. "By sitting in the tack room while we're all in the house? Or did you know I'd be doing night check?"

"I didn't. But I hoped you would. I left you a small present."

"You did? That's so thoughtful." She looked around.

Fred smiled. "Look in your riding helmet."

Bird chuckled. "Very clever." She turned over her helmet and lifted out a small box. "Dad, I didn't know you'd be here, and I didn't ..."

"Hush. I want nothing and need nothing. This is a family memory for you."

Bird unwrapped a delicate gold chain with a tiny horseshoe hanging from it. "It's gorgeous," she gasped.

Fred helped her fasten it around her neck. "It was my mother's."

Bird spun to look at him. "Your mother's? I don't know anything about her. She must have loved horses, too. Tell me about her!"

"It's a long story, and not without sadness. I will tell you all about her at the right time."

"I want to know her story. I don't care how long it takes."

Fred didn't speak. There was an uncomfortable pause. Bird didn't know her father well, but she knew him well enough to know that he could not be persuaded to talk about anything unless he wanted to.

Fred broke the silence. "Eva has spoken about her childhood trauma, is that it?"

Bird gasped. "How did you know?"

Fred nodded. "It was only a guess." He waited a beat. "It had to come out sometime. She's always known, but never shared. She tried to hide it behind all the protective layers she created."

Alec reacted. "That makes sense."

"You can help her," said Fred, "by believing in her. She has a lot of hard work to do."

Bird said, "You are wise, Dad. As wise as Mrs. Pierson."

Fred shook his head. "I know this from my mother's history. She was in a residential school. A person pays heavily for wisdom."

Bird had learned about residential schools in class. For decades, aboriginal children in Canada were taken from their parents by the government and forced to live in schools far away from home. In a disastrous program, with no insight into the consequences, they were forced to learn English ways, and they were not allowed to speak their native tongue or to learn about their own cultures. Some of the children died trying to get home. Physical, sexual, and mental abuse occurred, and lifetime scarring affected subsequent generations. Even when there was evidence that the program was failing, the government turned a blind eye.

Bird felt sadness for Fred's mother — her grandmother, whom she'd never known. The three were silent for a spontaneous moment of tribute to the heavy price of wisdom. She asked quietly, "One day, will you tell me about her?"

"One day I'll tell you. That is a promise."

Bird nodded, then said, "Come to the house with us. Please, Dad? Mrs. Pierson would love to see you, and Hannah, too, and Paul and Julia."

Fred gave her a sideways look. "But Eva? How do you think she would feel?"

Bird considered this. Her mother had always been bitter at Fred for leaving her pregnant so many years ago. All Bird's life, she'd heard from Eva about the rotten, no good, "Indian Cowboy" who was her father. Just before he died, Pete Pierson told them the urgent reason Fred had left all those years before. Fred was an RCMP undercover officer working on a dangerous case, and his cover had been blown. Eva and their baby were in dire peril. His "death" was the only way they could be safe, but the secret had to be kept from Eva, as well.

Alec offered his thoughts. "I may be wrong, but I agree with Bird. I think you should come with us. This is a new beginning for Eva. It's Christmas, and Christmas is for families. And Fred is your father, Bird. I think it'd be good."

Fred had doubts. "I don't know. Perhaps Eva doesn't need another shock tonight."

"I don't know, either," said Bird honestly. "But it would be really nice, and there's lots of food. Have you eaten?"

"No. Now that you ask, I'm very hungry." His face lit up as he changed the subject. "But come with me. You'll be happy to learn something." Fred left the tack room and began to walk down the stable aisle with purpose. "Something special."

"I thought *you* were the special present that Cody was talking about," Bird said, keeping up with his long strides.

Alec threw up his hands. "The coyote? You two speak a totally different language than me!"

Bird and Fred laughed, knowing full well that Alec was quite correct. In fact, aside from herself and her father, Bird knew of no other person who could speak to animals.

Fred stopped at Moonlight Sonata's stall. He leaned on the door and glanced at Bird before addressing the mare. *It's time to share your secret. Do you want to tell her, Moonie? Or shall I?*

Moonie shook her head up and down. *May I?*

Yes.

I will be having a foal when the new grass grows.

Moonie, enthused Bird. *This is wonderful news! Are you feeling all right?*

Yes. Very healthy.

Is the foal a good one?

Yes. It's a colt. He's very good, with long legs like his father.

Yes? And who is the father?

Dancer, of course. This is the foal we conceived on the day of the Good Man's funeral.

Bird was thrilled. She would need to explain this carefully to Moonie's owners, her friend Kimberly and her mother, Lavinia Davies. They hadn't expected their horse to miss a show season, and they also might not want the expense of a foal. Hannah might be a little upset, too. An unexplained "accident" like this surprise pregnancy would make her stable look somewhat lax.

"Can someone tell me what the horse is saying?" Alec asked. "I'm at a disadvantage here, not speaking Animal."

"Moonie's in foal with Dancer!" enthused Bird. "This is wonderful news."

"Wow," said Alec. "How did that happen?"

Fred had a joke at his expense. "I'll have to sit you down and fill you in on the birds and the bees, son."

Alec chortled, and asked, "Isn't Dancer Sundancer's father?"

Bird nodded. "Yes, he is."

Just then, Cliff entered the barn. He called, "Hello?"

Bird answered, "Cliff! We're in the arena aisle!"

"I was on my way to talk to Hannah and saw the lights. All good here? No problems?"

"Totally good. And we have news!"

Cliff came around the corner and saw Fred. "Well, Fred Sweetree! Good to see you, man!"

"Cliff. Good to see you!" They shook hands. The men had worked very closely together the previous summer.

"Cliff," said Bird. "Moonie's in foal!"

"No way." Cliff looked puzzled. He marched up to Moonie's stall and opened the door. He checked her milk sacs and belly. "Well, well. And I just told Kimberly to keep her mare more fit. How the heck did this happen?"

Alec nudged Cliff. "I'll have to sit you down and fill you in on the birds and the bees."

Fred smiled.

"Ha ha. Very funny." Cliff groaned at Alec's joke as he scratched his head. "We watch these horses carefully. The Davies didn't organize a breeding. They're going to go crazy."

"Not necessarily," said Fred. "How much is a breeding worth with Daring Dancer, the pride of Caledon?"

"He's the sire?" Cliff grinned and nodded his approval. "Right on. Three grand or more."

Bird said, "Tell Lavinia that she just saved herself three thousand dollars plus all the vet fees, and she'll have a mighty fine foal, to boot."

"You tell Lavinia," Cliff retorted. "That woman scares me."

"You said my mother scares you."

"Eva? Yes, she does. But in a contest, Lavinia scares me more."

Bird shrugged. "Lavinia loves Sunny. Remember? She wanted to buy him for Kimberly. Tell her Moonie is going to give her a foal just like him."

"If it's so easy, you do it." Then Cliff said to them all, "You can save me a trip. Tell Hannah we're going to light the bonfire and roast marshmallows. Come over and join us."

"Great idea!" said Bird. "It's just what we need to cheer everybody up. When should we show up?"

"I'm going to light it now. Bring everybody, okay?"

Bird turned to Fred. "Please stay. I'll make you a huge plate of turkey dinner and even warm it up."

"Which is better than I got," quipped Alec.

Bird begged, "Please?"

"Okay. But I'll take off quickly if my presence upsets Eva."

"That's a deal."

"I'll go with you now, Cliff, to get the fire lit properly." Fred winked at Cliff, pulled his cap out of his pocket, and put it on.

Bird said, "See you in a few minutes. This'll be fun!"

"Follow the flames," he said. "Over by the pond."

Cliff and Fred left the barn together.

"Too bad Mrs. Pierson hurt her ankle," said Alec. "She can't come to the bonfire, and she loves parties."

"Wait a minute! She *can* come to the party!" Bird rushed to Sundancer's stall.

Sunny? Do you want to come to a party? There'll be food.

Hmm. Apple cider?

Yes. And marshmallows.

What are we waiting for!

You can pull the sled again.

You didn't tell me that part.

For apple cider and marshmallows, would you do it? Mrs. Pierson needs a lift to the bonfire.

Okay. I'll do it for the Good Lady. And cider and marshmallows.

Thank you, Sunny.

"Hey, Alec," said Bird. "We have a plan. Can you tell everybody what's up and organize a plate of food for my father? Tell them to dress warmly. I'll get Sunny hitched up and bring him to the front door."

"He's going to pull Mrs. Pierson?"

"Yes!"

"Genius. I'll make sure she's got warm clothes and blankets."

Bird impulsively threw her arms around Alec's neck and gave him an enormous kiss on the lips. "Thank you."

Alec returned the kiss and tightened his embrace. They stood leaning into each other, forgetting the outside world, transported into a delicious alternate reality.

Hello-oo-oo? Sunny messaged. *What about the apple cider?*

Bird chuckled. Alec looked at her with dreamy eyes.

"Later," she said. "We have a Christmas to save!"

Once Alec had left the barn, Bird picked up the bag of treats that she'd left in the tack room. They were the size of golf balls, made of oats and crunch, and carrot and apple bits mixed with molasses. She'd baked them herself as her gift to the horses.

She was happy to have this time alone in the barn. First thing, she mixed one treat in a cup of hot water and let it sit. This was for Josh because he was very old and had trouble swallowing. The last thing Bird wanted was to kill the lovely white thoroughbred in a choking fit on Christmas.

She started at the front and worked her way down one aisle and up the next, having brief conversations with each horse as she went.

For the most part, the horses were happy with their lives, and wished Bird a Merry Christmas. Pastor was ready to get back in the show ring. Sabrina made a wish that she'd be champion pony again this coming season. Tall Sox thanked Bird for rescuing him and was pleased that he'd seen Fred tonight, to thank him, too. Charlie asked if Bird could get the massage person back because he was a little sore on his withers, and Bird made a mental note to check the fit of his saddle. Simon was so glad to get a treat that he had nothing to say at all, and Annie snatched it from her hand and messaged, *I should've been first!* Bird chortled at her impatience. Each horse was different, and she loved them all.

When she got to Amigo, the young thoroughbred had something on his mind.

Bird, you saved me last year from that dark place.

Yes, I remember, Amigo. You were very weak.

I was going to die. I had made peace with the Creator.

I'm glad you spoke up before I took the other horses from the shed that night.

It was my last chance.

You've grown big, now, and you're strong, Amigo.

Yes. Now, I'm ready to work for a living. Can you train me soon? I'll wear the saddle and the bridle, and do everything you ask. I've been watching and learning.

Bird was touched by his earnest request. *Yes, Amigo. I will start tomorrow if you think you're ready.*

I am! I will put the saddle on myself if you teach me how!

Bird chuckled. *If I can teach you that, we'll become famous.*

I want to be famous! Like Sundancer and Tall Sox.

Let's start slow, Amigo, and find out what you're best at.

The young grey horse nodded his head vigorously. *I want to be good at everything!*

Then you might well become an event horse.

What is that?

A horse that is good at dressage, show jumping, and jumping solid jumps across big open fields.

Yes! Yes! I can do all that! What is the first thing you said?

Dressage? It's like dancing.

Yes! I can dance! He lifted his feet in a jumble of steps.

Bird patted his head and laughed. *Okay. We start tomorrow.*

She moved on, distributing her Christmas treats, and thinking how lucky she was to be surrounded by so many good animals and good people. We're all mammals together on this Earth, she considered. We have to stand together, because what's good for one is good for the others. She remembered an old Cree prophecy:

> *When all the trees have been cut down,*
> *When all the animals have been hunted,*
> *When all the waters are polluted,*
> *When all the air is unsafe to breathe,*
> *Only then will you discover that you can't eat money.*

She brought Sunny out into the aisle and prepared him for the job at hand, with a surcingle around his chest and lunge lines to pull the sled.

Better than those old ropes, messaged Bird.

Anything is better than those old ropes. So itchy and smelly.

Alec opened the barn door and called, "Bird? Are you ready? Mrs. Pierson is bundled up and waiting."

"Almost!"

"Your mom and Stuart are coming, too!"

"Really? I thought they'd gone to bed."

"They had, but they say they wouldn't miss a bonfire."

"That's great." Bird felt a surge of hopefullness.

"Don't be too long. We have Christmas to save, remember?"

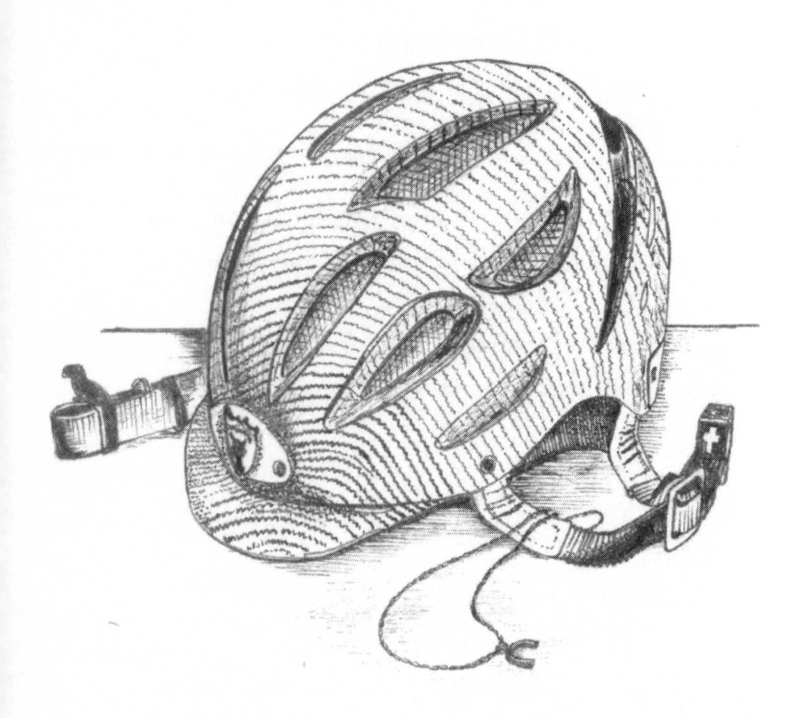

7 THE BONFIRE

Dashing through the snow,
In a one-horse open sleigh,
O'er the fields we go,
Laughing all the way …

Bird slogged beside Sunny as he calmly pulled the sleigh carrying Laura Pierson, wrapped in blankets and delighted with the plan.

"This time I'm going to enjoy the ride!" Mrs. Pierson called out. She pulled the blanket up to her ears and shook with merriment.

The top layer of ice had melted, and the snow beneath their feet was heavy, but their mood was light as they moved toward the party. Alec and Julia walked on either side of Mrs. Pierson.

The moon climbed high over the dripping, ice-laden treetops, and mist rose from the pond. As the air continued to warm in the southerly breeze, the melting icicles tinkled like music.

"Isn't it beautiful?" Mrs. Pierson sighed.

"Like a magical kingdom!" exclaimed Julia.

The closer they got to the fire, the more intense was the aroma of burning wood, and the louder the sounds of crackling and snapping as flames ate up the small branches before settling in to dwell in the large logs.

Alec and Julia joined Mrs. Pierson in the singing of "Joy to the World." They sang loudly and out of tune. Mrs. Pierson shrieked with fits of the giggles as they bumped over ice ridges.

Bird remembered how much pain Mrs. Pierson had suffered just the night before. What a difference a day makes, she thought. And Paul's veterinary medicine.

Excuse me? You said there was apple cider?

Yes, Sunny. Apple cider and marshmallows. Soon.

Bird saw Fred sitting on a lawn chair in the shadows, digging into a plate of food. At least he'll have had some dinner, thought Bird, if he has to leave early.

Paul waved to them and motioned that he needed some help, so Alec and Julia ran off to carry chairs and set them up far enough away from the fire to be safe. Hannah and Paul were busy organizing the rum and cider. Cliff and his son were cutting sticks to roast marshmallows, while Cliff's daughter played with the children and kept them safe.

Stuart and Eva were sitting together hand in hand, looking into the fire. She took a closer look. What the heck was Eva wearing? She was in an old plaid coat and a grey hat with earflaps, clothes she'd never seen her mother wear. This was a surprise. At least Eva was warm, she thought. Much warmer than the flimsy outfits she normally wore.

In the glow of the flames, she saw a little smile on Eva's face. Bird felt a pang of optimism.

Don't get too close to the fire, Bird.

No worries there, Sunny.

I don't want my coat singed.

I don't want that, either. I had my hair singed off once already.

I remember that. You looked bad.

But I saved those horses from the fire.

Yes. But you looked bad for a very long time.

Such a pal, Sunny. Bird laughed out loud.

Mrs. Pierson called to her from the sled. "I know just how you feel, dear! Isn't this wonderful?"

"Yes, it's wonderful," answered Bird. And it was. Suddenly, Bird felt better about Christmas. Take away the fuss of gift buying, parties, preparing feasts, and travel plans, and remove the false expectations of non-stop happiness and family perfection. Take all the stress away, and unexpectedly you find the simple pleasures of being with the people you love. Not just my family, Bird thought, but the families of people I care about.

And gifts feel so good to give, she thought, reliving Hannah and Julia's delight in her small gifts. Not for their lavishness, but for their thoughtfulness, showing that she cared.

A red van came to a stop in the field, followed by a black one, then a white one.

Mrs. Pierson called out, "Bird! Stop!"

"Whoa, Sunny," said Bird. "What's wrong, Mrs. Pierson?"

"Nothing's wrong! Everything's right! My boys are here with their families! Turn left! Drive me over!"

Sunny pulled Mrs. Pierson over the field, toward the cars.

"Here they are! All of them. Bless their dear souls!" The elderly woman was so excited that Bird worried she might jump out, swollen ankle and all. "Faster, Sunny!"

"Mrs. Pierson! Stay where you are!"

"Giddy-up!" the old woman yelled.

Sundancer picked up a trot and covered the ground quickly. Bird ran to keep up and stood with him while the van doors slid open. Mrs. Pierson's three sons and their wives, plus their grown children and some cousins with their kids, came tumbling out. Eighteen adults and three small boys.

They embraced each other heartily and laughed and told jokes. Mrs. Pierson was swept up in their excitement, and Bird was astonished by the sheer amount of love and goodwill they conveyed.

The Pierson men lifted Mrs. Pierson from the sled and carried her to a place by the fire, where the whole family could spend some time.

"Thank you Bird, dear!" Mrs. Pierson waved and called as she was transported. "You saved my life! And thank you, dear, dear Sundancer!"

One of the women turned and regarded Sunny. Her look was appraising and appreciative.

That one. She knows me.

She seems to, Sunny. Do you know her?

No. But I want to.

Bird felt a tug on her coat and looked down. One of the little boys had remained with her. He looked up at her shyly and tilted his head. She guessed he was about five years old.

"Hello," Bird said. "What's your name?"

"Henry."

"Hi, Henry. Welcome to Christmas at Saddle Creek."

Henry looked at the horse. He took off a mitten, then reached up and placed his small hand on Sunny's nose, right between his nostrils, and held it there.

Sunny stood very still. *I like this boy. He's smart. He's trying to understand me.*

I see that. Can you give him a ride in the sled?

Yes.

"Henry, would you like to sit in the sled, like your great-grandmother did, and go for a ride?" Bird asked.

"Yes!" Henry turned and sped away as fast as he could.

Bird was surprised. *I thought he said yes.*

Children are interesting. Here he comes again.

Bird saw three little boys hurtling toward them. *Now I understand! He brought the others.*

He's a thoughtful boy. But I'm not giving them rides if I don't like them.

They're good kids, Sunny.

Hmph. I'll be the judge. Some small humans are horrible.

It'll be really bad if we give one a ride and not the others.

That would be their problem, not mine.

The boys stopped running and stared at Sunny. Aside

from five-year-old Henry, Bird saw that one was about eight years old, and the other maybe two.

"Hi," she said. "My name is Bird. What's yours?"

"I'm Luke," said the oldest. "I learned to ride on a pony named Robyn. My teacher taught me lots of fun things, like trotting around the arena, making words from letters on the wall, and picking up things and putting them down somewhere else." He was excited and talking fast, but suddenly stopped and looked at Sunny. "Wow. You are beautiful."

Okay. He passes. I'll give him a ride.

"What's his name?" asked Luke.

"Sundancer."

"Really? You mean the famous jumping horse that goes so high, and nobody can beat him, and he gets all the trophies?"

So, what are we waiting for, Bird? The kid's a genius.

What about the small one?

Before Sunny could reply, Mrs. Pierson's two-year-old great-grandson said, "Me Dwakie." He stretched up his arms to Bird.

Luke said, "His name is Drake. He's our cousin."

"Thanks, Luke. Hello, Drake. Do you want up?"

"Yes, pweese!"

Bird bent down and raised him from the ground. Drake's little body twisted until he was at Sunny's face. His small mittened hand patted the big horse's forehead.

"Up!" the boy said, and pointed to Sunny's back.

May I? asked Bird.

Certainly. This kid is brave, and he knows what he wants.

Okay. Bird placed him on Sunny's back. She tucked his toes securely under the straps and showed him how to hold the rope between the rings of the surcingle.

Bird was satisfied that the child was safe. *Tell me if you want him off.*

I don't. He's happy up there.

Bird could see that Sunny was right. The little boy was smiling and perfectly content.

"Luke and Henry?" Bird said. "Get in the sled, and we'll go for a ride. Drake can sit up here, okay?"

The two boys jumped in the sled, and off they went.

A little late, Bird thought about asking their parents if it was okay. If not, she'd have a lot of explaining to do.

She needn't have worried. As she neared the adults, the horse and sleigh parade got an exuberant round of applause. The parents jumped up from their chairs and took pictures. They made a big fuss over their kids, with shouts of, "This is fantastic!" and, "Isn't this great!"

Mrs. Pierson called out, "That's my girl, Bird, dear! What fun!"

Cliff's son, Seb, ran over with his little boy, who was likely three. "Room for one more?" he asked Bird.

Sunny? Okay with you?

Sunny took a good look at the new child.

"I'm Brent!" said the little boy. "Nice horsey! Please can I come, too?"

He passes. Put him on the sled.

Thanks, Sunny.

Bird answered, "Sure, Seb! Tuck Brent in, and off we go!"

Now there were three boys on the sled and one on the horse.

Still okay, Sunny?

I never thought I'd give pony rides.

You're good at it.

Don't expect me to do it again.

You're such a fake. You're having fun.

Sunny snorted and nickered. *I admit it.*

Bird checked that little Drake was still smiling, which he was, then looked back to see the others in the sled. Eight-year-old Luke sat behind his little brother, Henry, and held him with both arms. Little Brent sat wide-eyed in front, held by the little arms of Henry.

"Are you guys okay back there?" she asked.

"Yes!" they answered in unison and nodded their heads enthusiastically. "Let's go!"

Bird led Sunny around the field. It was the perfect vantage point to witness the ever-changing dynamic of the party.

The great fire burned with a life of its own, flicking serpent tongues of flame up into the air. The stars twinkled above them, and the moon was full, bathing the icy fields around them in a soft white glow. Steam rose from the pond, adding a mystical touch. Bird hoped that someone was taking pictures of all this beauty.

She looked for her father. He was her one concern. Fred had not been sure of his welcome, and neither was she. Then, she spotted him. He was sitting with Mrs. Pierson. Bird relaxed. Mrs. Pierson had a hand on Fred's sleeve, deep in serious conversation.

Cliff had brought his guitar, and people had gathered to sing Christmas carols. Strains of "Silent Night," "We Three Kings," and "Rudolph the Red-Nosed Reindeer" drifted across the fields and echoed in the woods, creating a delayed reverberation to the music.

Marshmallows were roasted, and cider was offered. There were coolers filled with beer and wine for the adults, and water and pop for the kids. Hannah had brought out all the leftovers from dinner, and people were making sandwiches on the table that Paul and Cliff had hauled from the garage.

Bird watched as Fred stood and walked up to Eva and Stuart. She held her breath and slowed Sunny's pace so she could observe. Stuart got to his feet. Both men appeared relaxed. Stuart motioned to the chair beside Eva, and Fred sat down. Bird couldn't hear the words, but she didn't need to. Eva seemed at ease. Maybe Alec was right, that this night was a new beginning for her mother. Bird crossed her fingers under her mittens. It sure would make life less complicated if they could all get along.

Bird continued to walk beside her horse, one hand on little Drake's leg, just in case he decided to squirm. Happy noises and laughter filled the air, and Bird felt a stirring of what she imagined was the Christmas spirit.

Alec walked toward them across the field, carrying a hot cup of cider and a perfectly cooked marshmallow. "I made it just for you," he said. "I burned about a dozen, so I had to eat them myself."

"Thanks!" Bird took them from him gratefully. "Will you be upset if I give these to Sunny? I promised, in payment for pulling the sled."

"Of course you did. Why didn't I guess?"

"Seriously."

"No problem. I'll go get some more. Be right back!"

If you'd gobbled up my marshmallow and drank my cider ...

But I didn't, did I?

Bird held out her palm with the perfect sugary treat. All the kids watched as Sunny sniffed it and touched it with his lips to check the temperature. They squealed and giggled as he licked it, then picked it up carefully with his teeth. He slowly savoured it. He nodded his head, smacked his lips, then flipped his upper lip over his nostrils and made a loud sniffing noise.

Very nice. I'll need one more.

First, have some cider.

Bird held the cup in front of him.

"Is he going to actually drink that?" asked Luke.

"Yes. He loves apples, and cider is made of apples."

"But how can he drink from a cup?" asked Henry, furrowing his brow.

"Just watch."

The boys scrambled out of the sled and stared with eyes wide as Sunny stuck his tongue into the cup and slurped it up. Bird put the last drops on her hand and let him lick them off.

"Cool!" said Henry.

"I want some, too!" said Brent.

Just then, one of Mrs. Pierson's sons came striding from the fire to get the children. "Who wants to cook a marshmallow?" he called.

"Me!" yelled Luke, who raced to him. "Can I do it myself, Papu?"

"And me, too, Papu?" Henry copied.

"Me, too, Pa … pu?" mimicked Drake. He enunciated the words carefully, which made everybody laugh.

"Yes to everybody. Yes, yes, yes you can. Everybody can cook their own."

He gently began to lift Drake down from the back of the horse. Drake's face clouded, and he held the straps more tightly. Bird thought he was about to resist.

"Drake?" asked his grandfather. "Would you like to see Mommy and Daddy?"

Drake's face brightened, and he let go of the horse, but threw his body around to pat Sunny on the way down.

"Nice horse!" he said.

See, Bird? messaged Sunny. *I told you they were good kids.*

"Thanks, Bird," Mrs. Pierson's son said. "You created a great memory for these kids. One they'll never forget."

Bird said, "It was fun for me, too, and for Sunny." She patted his neck.

Easy for you to say. I did all the pulling.

Sunny's job was done, and Bird and her horse began their walk back to the barn.

You made those kids happy tonight, Sunny.

It wasn't as bad as I thought it'd be.

You're a grinch. A nice grinch, but a grinch.

As they went, Bird watched the four small boys and Mrs. Pierson's tall son as they headed back to the bonfire to join the party, their bodies silhouetted by the flames. A dog came running to join them.

It was Lucky, dashing to greet them with his tail wagging, ears flopping, and tongue lolling. He loved children, and he kept them from straying. Bird smiled. He was a simple dog, but he took his job seriously, even if the adults didn't know they needed his watchful patrol.

From afar, the celebration looked like a scene from a hundred years ago or more. Under her breath, Bird whispered, "I think I get Christmas."

8 VOWS

Joyful all ye nations rise,
Join the triumph of the skies …

After settling Sunny in his stall, and giving one last pat to each of the twenty horses, Bird walked back to the fire. She looked over the fields and noticed that several more cars had joined the vans belonging to Mrs. Pierson's sons. Trucks and cars and Skidoos were lined up in a row, and people of all ages were heading to the action.

It was starting to look like a fall fair, she thought. There must be more than fifty people, and another car was driving in, followed by a truck. Good thing Sunny was back in the barn. He would've gone on strike with all those kids to pull in the sled.

She was shocked by a deep voice beside her. "Hello?"

Bird jumped away.

"I didn't mean to startle you."

"You scared me out of my wits!"

"I'm so sorry. I'm Tom Francis, the pastor of your grandmother's church."

Bird was confused. Jean's church? Then she took another look at the man. "Tom, the hydro man? Of Bob and Tom?"

"Yes! The hydro man."

"Who got a scare from the coyote under the covers?"

Tom laughed. "This wasn't intended as payback. I'm sorry."

Bird regained her composure as her heart began to beat normally. "It's okay. I didn't expect anyone to be here."

"Your grandmother told us to come back if we were free. I hope you don't mind that we're taking you up on that, and we brought the families, too. They wanted to come."

Bird gazed at the gathering crowd. "Your families are very welcome. 'The more the merrier,' as Aunt Hannah says! And Mrs. Pierson's not my grandmother, she's a really good friend."

"And a really nice lady." Tom looked back at the crowd. "Hey, it looks great, with the bonfire and everything, eh?"

"Yeah, it does. Where did all these people come from?"

"I've talked to some of them. Mostly neighbours who were driving back from dinner and stopped when they saw the fire. It's such a nice night, they don't want to go home. What a change of weather, eh?"

"For sure. Are the hydro lines up and working?"

"Yup. We finished about an hour ago. Just in time to pick up the wife and kids. And Bob's with us, too. And his mother, Gladys, who's alone now and loves a party."

Bird nodded, but she'd stopped listening. An incredibly interesting idea began to percolate in her brain. "Reverend Francis, can we talk?"

Tom was surprised. "Of course."

Back at the fire, Bird sat down on one of the bales of straw that Cliff had brought over in his truck. Tom Francis had agreed to her plan. Actually he was delighted. He left his wife and kids with Bob and his mother at the fire, and he drove home to get things organized.

Bird hoped that it would turn out the way she imagined.

"Hey, Bird," called Paul, ladling out cider from the bottom of the pot. "Can you help Hannah get more cider from the house? We're running out."

"No problem!" Bird headed to the kitchen.

Hannah was already there. "We're out of cups and marshmallows, and rum and cider," she said. "No stores are open, and people keep coming!"

"Why don't we bring the last of our beer and wine and pop?"

"We're all out of that, too."

Bird shrugged. "It's not like we invited all these people to show up."

"I know, but I hate to run out of things. The only thing we have is champagne."

"Champagne?"

"It's been in the basement for years, waiting for the right occasion."

"That's weird, just so you know. Aunt Hannah, let's go back to the fire. If we're out of everything, we're out."

"Bird, you make perfect sense. And we're definitely out!"

Fifteen minutes later, Paul stood on a bale of straw and cleared his throat. "Hello, folks!" he said as loudly as he could.

Nobody could hear him, and the noise continued just as loudly as before.

"Hello!" Paul yelled again, with no result.

Bird grabbed the ladle and started banging it as hard as she could on the empty iron pot.

The metal-on-metal racket got people's attention.

"Thanks, Bird." Paul began again. "Merry Christmas to you all — family, friends, neighbours. Welcome to Saddle Creek Farm on this beautiful night. I'm sorry to say, though, that we've run out of absolutely everything."

Immediately, there was a flood of offers. "Why didn't you say so!" said Rob from next door. "I have a car full of beer!"

Brian said, "I'll be right back with some wine and chips!"

"I have a case of ginger ale and boxes of Girl Guide cookies!" offered Jirina. "Just across the road!"

"Excuse me!" Mrs. Pierson slowly stood up with the help of one of her sons. "Before you go scurrying away to get things, and how lovely of you all to pitch in, I have something to ask."

People hushed to listen.

"May I talk, dear?" she asked Paul. "Is that all right?"

"Yes, yes, of course. Whatever you do is all right with me."

"Thank you, dear." She cleared her throat. Another son stood to help, and she held on to both men. "This is the first Christmas without my dear Pete, and I miss him more than I can say. You all knew him, and I know you miss him, too. He was thankful for his long and full life, and I feel blessed that I had him in mine for so many years." Her throat constricted with sentiment, and she needed a moment before she continued.

"Pete's here with us tonight. I feel his loving and generous spirit. So, surrounded by family and kind people doing kind things, could you raise your eyes to the heavens with me and wish Pete a Merry Christmas?"

Every single person, young and old, looked up at the full moon and the twinkling stars.

As if on cue, a shooting star trailed across the sky.

The audible gasp was spontaneous and emotional. If a person wanted a sign that the universe sometimes listens, that was it.

In the ensuing silence, Tom Francis arrived in his car. He rolled down his window and gave Bird a thumbs-up.

Perfect timing, Bird thought.

Mrs. Pierson raised her hands. "I would not have been here, if not for this dear girl." She pointed at Bird. "Bird, dear, come up here beside me." She smiled with twinkling eyes and gestured.

Bird stood up in front of the crowd, embarrassed.

"A tree crashed through my roof last night, and I was injured badly and very cold. This dear, dear girl arrived at my house with her wonderful Sundancer and her magical Cody. They carried me here through that wicked storm. I would've died but for her." Mrs. Pierson hugged Bird close to her chest. "Thank you, dear Bird," she whispered.

Bird answered truthfully, "Really, thanks are to Cody and Sunny."

Mrs. Pierson's sons helped her back to her chair and elevated her ankle on a bale of straw. People began to mill around.

Tom had parked and was walking toward them quickly.

Bird knew that she needed to hold the crowd's attention. She said, with excitement in her voice, "Folks, please stay where you are because something else is about to happen. A big surprise."

People murmured and whispered to each other.

"What are you talking about, Bird?" asked Paul.

Bird smiled mysteriously. "You have no idea how special this night will become. May I introduce Reverend Tom Francis."

Tom stepped up onto a bale. He held a large black leather folder, and he had changed into his black robe and white collar. He appeared very different than when in his hydro work clothes.

"Thank you, Bird. Good evening to you all. I am here to perform a sacred and beautiful ceremony. Will Ms. Hannah Bradley and Dr. Paul Daniels come forward?"

Hannah and Paul were astounded. "What are you up to, Bird?" asked Hannah.

"Is it what I think it is?" Paul wanted to know.

Bird nodded. "Is it okay with you two? Because if it isn't ..."

"Yes. It is. It is more than okay." Hannah smoothed her hair off her face with her gloved hands and dusted off her coat.

Paul said, "It is a dream come true. We'll get the marriage licence first thing next week." He took Hannah's hand tightly in his. Together they stepped forward.

"I need Mrs. Eva Gilmour, and her daughters, Ms. Alberta and Ms. Julia Simms. I also need ..." Tom paused and motioned to Bird to come closer. "Who should be the groomsmen?" he whispered in her ear.

Bird didn't hesitate. "Stuart Gilmour and Alec Daniels."

"I also need Stuart Gilmour and Alec Daniels. Please come up here!"

As the wedding party assembled, Bird snuck down to talk to Mrs. Pierson. "Can we borrow one of your beautiful rings?" she asked. Mrs. Pierson always wore five or six. "I'll bring it right back."

"Of course, dear! But do not return it. I want this to be Hannah's wedding ring, and I'll tell her to leave it to you when she dies." She had already twisted a ring off her knobby finger, and now she placed the antique in Bird's palm.

"You knew, didn't you? That there'd be a wedding?"

"You can't fool an old fooler," Mrs. Pierson laughed, then added, "You must only fool people for good reasons, not for bad."

As soon as Cliff had realized what was happening, he'd hurried back to his house and returned with a music system. It was an old cassette player and an even older speaker, but when he turned it on, the music quality was surprisingly good. The first song he played was by the Beatles: "When I'm Sixty-Four."

Hannah and Paul laughed. Hannah said, "Well, I guess that's pretty close." They began to waltz to the song.

Reverend Francis called it to a halt. "Not yet! We dance after the vows, not before. And whatever you do, don't kiss the bride!"

Chaos followed, and Bird realized that she needed to get people organized. She placed Hannah and Paul together in the middle, in front of Tom Francis, with their backs to the fire. She asked Eva to stand at Hannah's right side, with Julia on Eva's right.

Eva whispered, "I can't believe I'm Hannah's matron of honour in this outfit!"

Bird chuckled. "You've never looked better." She adjusted an earflap as if it were an expensive fascinator. "Love the hat." Then, Bird looked directly at her mother. "Are you okay, Mom?"

"I'm okay. And so happy that my big sister is marrying such a good man." She touched Bird's cheek. "Can we talk later?"

Bird gulped with surprise. This was new territory for their relationship. She nodded with apprehension. "Okay. Later."

She moved Stuart to stand beside Paul's left, and she put Mrs. Pierson's ring in his hand. "Don't lose it," she cautioned. "It's Mrs. Pierson's." Stuart nodded solemnly.

Beside him on his left, already in place, Alec stood grinning. "Beat you to it!" he joked. "You're such a boss. I like it."

Bird winked at him, and then spoke to Tom. "Okay, Reverend Francis, get going!" She slipped in to take her place at Julia's right.

He opened his folder and began to read. "Dearly Beloved, we are gathered here to join together this man and this woman in holy matrimony. It is not to be entered into lightly, but reverently, discreetly, advisedly, and solemnly. If any person can show just cause why they may not be joined together, let them speak now or forever hold their peace."

There was complete silence as he looked around expectantly. Bird noted that there was always a little suspense at this time of a wedding service.

"Hi, Bird!" yelled a little voice.

"Hi, Henry!" she whispered back.

"Henry!" whispered Luke loudly. "You're not supposed to talk!" Their mother laughed as she hugged her boys.

Reverend Francis began to speak again. "We are here today to witness the joining in marriage of Paul Daniels and Hannah Bradley. This occasion marks the celebration of love and commitment with which this man and this woman begin their life together, in one of the holiest of bonds."

He paused for effect. "This is a beginning and a continuation of their growth as individuals. With mutual care, respect, responsibility, and knowledge comes the affirmation of each one's own life, happiness, growth, and freedom. With respect for individual boundaries comes the freedom to love unconditionally. The emotional safety of a loving relationship becomes the fertile soil of continued growth. With care and responsibility toward self and one another comes the potential for full and happy lives."

Bird leaned forward and said to Reverend Francis, "Are we doing the long or the short version?"

The reverend looked startled. He leafed through the pages and skipped forward.

"Do you, Paul Daniels, take Hannah Bradley to be your wife?"

Paul gazed at Hannah with glowing eyes. "I will."

"Do you wish to say anything at this time?"

"Yes, I do. I've been practising my vows for a long time. I wrote them down but don't happen to have them with me." He patted his pockets just in case. "I'll try my best."

People chuckled, but grew quiet as Paul took both of Hannah's hands in his. "Hannah, you are my world.

I love you, I cherish you, I cannot live without you. I will be there with you in good times and in bad. I will protect you and comfort you and honour you always." His eyes were full of love. "In fact … nothing makes any sense without you. I vow to be the best I can be for you, for as long as we both shall live."

Hannah wiped her cheeks with the back of her hand and snuffled.

The Reverend said, "Do you, Hannah Bradley, take Paul Daniels to be your husband?"

Hannah nodded and smiled, then croaked loudly, "Yes!"

Everyone laughed with delight at her enthusiasm.

Reverend Francis waved his hands and hushed them. "Do you wish to say anything at this time?"

Hannah sniffed, and inhaled deeply. "Yes. I do. Thank you." Her mouth quivered. "I haven't practised, so I hope this comes out right." She squared her shoulders. "Paul, you taught me what love means. I didn't know. I didn't know what it was and really, I didn't know I needed it. So I pushed it away. I guess … I guess I was guarding myself, maybe from hurt, and protecting myself. But you were patient, Paul. You stayed. And you taught me. So now … now I belong with you. And I promise to be my best self and to give you my best self, for as long as we both shall live."

Paul and Hannah hugged each other for a long moment.

The reverend asked, "Is there a ring?"

Bird nodded and pointed to Stuart, who held it up.

Reverend Francis motioned to Stuart to give the ring to Paul, and he cleared his throat. "Paul, say after me ..."

Paul politely raised a hand. He said, "I'd like to do this, thank you. I've practised this part, too." He faced Hannah and said earnestly, "The shape of a ring has no beginning and no end, which makes it a symbol of eternity. A *wedding* ring is a symbol of love. Therefore, I give you this ring as a token of my love, for all eternity. Hannah, with this ring I thee wed." Paul gently slipped Mrs. Pierson's ring on Hannah's finger.

Tears flowed down Hannah's face. She was overwhelmed with emotion. Bird thought she wouldn't be able to continue.

But Hannah surprised her. She held Paul's gaze and haltingly said, "Paul, I, I don't have a ring to give you. But ... I give you my heart ... and my mind ... and my whole self. You are my only love, and my best friend. You are my ... confidant and my consoler. With my ... soul, I thee wed."

There was a sigh of approval as Hannah raised herself on her toes, and Paul leaned down slightly. They kissed each other tenderly and lengthily.

"Not yet!" Tom Francis said, but as the kiss continued, he was drowned out by gales of laughter. He quickly shouted, "By the power vested in me, I now pronounce you husband and wife. You may now kiss the bride!"

With perfect timing, Fred rolled up in his truck with Cliff on the flatbed. They came to a stop beside the wedding party, lifted down a table with a white tablecloth, and then unloaded two heavy boxes.

Cliff hollered, "Champagne on ice! Come, bring your cup or find a used one! Let's drink to the health and happiness of the newly married couple."

Hannah winked at Bird. "Now, *this* is the right occasion."

The party began. Music blared from the little speaker hooked up to the generator, and people danced and sang along to the familiar tunes of the Rolling Stones, John Denver, the Beach Boys, Roy Orbison, Three Dog Night, Queen, Eric Clapton, Carole King, and CCR, all picked by Cliff in a tribute to Hannah and Paul's generation.

Bird was pleased to see her mother, Eva, and Stuart dancing closely to "Rocky Mountain High." She made a wish that Eva would figure out how to trust people and somehow, someday, let go of the past. As she was making the wish, Eva caught her eye. She whispered something in Stuart's ear. Stuart nodded and looked at Bird. Eva walked toward her. Bird stayed where she was, unsure of what would follow, alert that Eva could erupt at any minute.

"I'm sorry I didn't give you a present, Bird." Her mother's eyes dropped to the ground. "I'm sorry about a lot of things." She looked up again. For the first time she could remember, Bird saw openness, honesty, and kindness in them. "Bird, I have a lot to make up for. Can we start again, if you'll forgive me?"

Bird nodded cautiously. "Yes, I'd like that, Mom, if we can start again. And I'm sorry for a whole lot of things, too. Like dressing up in the red sheet at dinner and mimicking you. That was awful. It started the whole thing."

Eva put her hand out and took Bird's. "If it did, I'm grateful to you. I'm glad it's finally out in the open." She held out her hand and opened her fingers. On her palm rested a shiny object, twinkling in the light of the fire. "Please accept this, my remarkable, brave daughter. Merry Christmas. May we have many more."

Bird was astonished. She lifted it off her mother's hand and gasped. It was a brooch with a rearing horse on it, made of silver. "This is beautiful!"

"Your father gave it to me on our very first date. I want you to have it."

"Thank you. Thank you so much." Bird was overwhelmed with gratitude and didn't know how to express herself. "I'll put it in a very special place for safekeeping, Mom. I'll keep it forever."

Eva's bottom lip quivered. Tears were ready to drop from her eyes. "I have much work to do to make up for everything, Bird. I know that. And I won't be perfect, believe me, but I vow to try."

Bird sniffed and nodded. "I'll try, too. And, Mom? You're the one who's brave. I didn't know about Granddad."

Eva said, "I never knew how to talk about it. It had to come out. And however that happened, I'm glad it did." She turned and slid into Stuart's welcoming arms. Stuart gave Bird a grateful look, and Eva smiled at her. "I love you, Bird," she said as they danced away.

Bird and Alec sat together on a bale of straw off to the side and watched as people enjoyed themselves.

"She told me she loved me," said Bird. "Twice in one day."

"You told me." He took her hand and traced the veins on the back of it. "Three times."

"But all my life ..."

"I know, Bird. She's been a wreck." Alec shook his head slowly. "This is hard. You can't expect her to change into a nice person overnight. It won't be easy, but I'll be right here for you every step."

"I know you will. Alec, what if you'd agreed that we should be just friends?"

He laughed. "No chance. But you were right that some people will judge."

"And you were right that we shouldn't care what they think."

He gave her shoulders a squeeze. "This is the best wedding ever. Look at how much fun people are having. Young and old, dancing and laughing."

"Yeah. It's very cool," agreed Bird. "Weren't their vows amazing? Aunt Hannah was crying. Paul was crying."

"You'll have to call him *Uncle* Paul, now."

"You're right. Aunt Hannah and Uncle Paul." She could get used to that. "I loved their wedding."

"You did that, Bird."

"Yeah, I guess I did. I'm more surprised than anyone."

"How did you even think of it?"

"I wouldn't have if Tom the hydro man weren't also the pastor of Mrs. Pierson's church."

"Do you think he really is?"

"What? You think he's a fraud?"

"Just saying."

Bird's eyes flicked back and forth with doubt. "He said he was a pastor."

"Do you believe everything you hear?"

"Mrs. Pierson recognized him!"

Alec's eyes danced. "The only thing we know for sure is that Mrs. Pierson's glasses are broken. She's blind as a bat."

"I hate you, Alec Daniels!" Bird and Alec fell into each other's arms, laughing. They couldn't help but find each other's lips.

9 THE CHRISTMAS MIRACLE

Star of wonder, star of light,
Star of royal beauty bright.

One kiss led to another. Alec and Bird felt magnetized, stuck together timelessly and blissfully. Bird wanted this embrace to last forever.

Bird girl. Emergency.

Cody? Not now.

The pond. NOW!

Bird jumped up from the bale of straw, knocking Alec backward to the ground.

"What!?" he yelled.

"Alec, the pond! Come with me!"

"What's up?"

Bird was gone. She ran as fast as she could. Weaving in and out of dancing couples, pushing down chairs, and leaping over straw bales, Bird elbowed her way past the big bonfire and straight to the pond.

Cody, I'm here.

Bird heard nothing back from him. She peered closely at the ice-covered pond and all around it.

Lucky came running with his nose to the ground. His tail was between his legs.

Lucky? What's wrong?

I lost him. Lost him. Little boy. Boy. Lucky pawed frantically at the ice at the edge of the pond and opened up some water.

Bird was horrified as it dawned on her that there was a boy under the ice. And from the way the ice splintered as Lucky clawed, the ice was soft, and the boy had fallen through. But where?

Distraught, Bird tried to pick up a signal from the boy as she frenetically looked for a clue. The pond was small. The weather change had made the snow around the pond mushy, and there were frozen reeds and bushes around it. It was hard to get a good look at where the child might have gone in.

Over there. She saw tracks. A line of small boot prints had sunk into the soft ice very slightly, where a child might have crossed the pond. They were covered by canine prints. Cody had tracked him. She followed the prints with her eyes. There! A hole!

Alec arrived, puffing.

"Alec! A kid is under there. We have to get him out. Get help!"

Without a word, Alec spun around and ran, calling, "Help! Help! A child fell through the ice!"

Bird rushed to the hole. It was at the far edge of the pond. She imagined the child's panic. He would be fighting for air and struggling to get out from under the ice.

Lucky kept up his frantic scratching.

Lucky, come over here.

He's not there now, not now.

Where is he?

Lucky sat up and sniffed in great concentration. *I do not know, not know.* He resumed his digging.

Cody? Where are you?

There was no communication from the small coyote.

Bird grabbed a thick fallen branch from the ground and began to pound at the ice. She thumped as hard as she could, hoping to crack it open.

Fred arrived with a spade. He began to chop and hack. *Alberta. A child is under there?*

Yes. Cody called to me less than a minute ago.

Cliff backed his truck up so he'd be ready to pull the child out. He attached a sturdy rope to the undercarriage and threw the other end to Fred. Fred nodded, understanding the intent.

Paul and Stuart came armed with whatever they could grab and pitched in, striking at the ice with great force. Alec, Tom, and Bob whacked at it with iron T-bars. Cliff handed ice picks to the Pierson men with their sons, who went at it with a vengeance, doing some serious damage to the icy surface.

The crowd moved from the fire to see what was going on. Hannah held them back with calm authority.

Bird recognized her horse-trainer voice. "Please, folks! Let them do their work!"

A shriek cut through the noise. "Henry!" followed by a desperate figure pushing through the people to get to the pond.

Bird saw Hannah stop the woman before she could jump in.

"It's Henry," cried his mother, frantic with fear. "I thought he was with the others. I lost sight of him. He was right beside me."

"How long ago?"

"Maybe a minute or two, not more."

"That's good," comforted Hannah. "He hasn't been under very long."

The young woman nodded, grasping at any good news. She sobbed in Hannah's arms, with Luke holding her legs tightly, trying to console her.

"Henry!" Luke yelled toward the pond. "Don't give up! You're my baby brother!"

The ice was more stubborn than Bird had at first judged, but all the bashing and chipping and smashing was succeeding in breaking through, and large cracks were forming.

Without warning, the whole surface gave way. A large piece sank, and water gushed up. The people watching gave a loud cheer, and all the workers renewed their efforts. Soon the pond looked like a patchwork quilt, with water lapping over chunks of ice as they rose and fell.

Lucky jumped in with a mighty leap. He dove and emerged, then dove again.

Bird girl, came a faint transmission. *Help us now.*

Cody! Where are you?

Under log, under ice.

Bird felt a cold sweat breaking out. They were trapped under a submerged log and couldn't swim out.

Lucky! Dive deeper!

Across from her, Bird saw Fred waving to get her attention.

Alberta, I'm going in with the rope. Tell Cliff to drive when I give you the order.

You heard Cody?

Yes. When I know where they are, I'll get them freed.

Bird rushed over to the truck to give Cliff instructions. From the corner of her eye, she saw her father throw off his coat and boots, and tie the rope around his waist, preparing to dive.

"Cliff!" Bird yelled. "Henry's stuck under a log. Fred will give me a signal, then you drive and pull them out."

Cliff nodded. He turned the ignition and awaited the order.

Fred intently studied the pond. He was crouched, ready to leap at the first sign of underwater movement.

All eyes were on the pond. The ice chunks and water became still as the chopping stopped. The only noise was the sound of Lucky splashing as he continued to surface, then dive again. It was seconds, but seemed a lifetime.

Fred saw bubbles. He jumped into the icy water.

Lucky began to whine and yip, louder and louder.

Lucky?

They're coming up! Coming up!

Good dog!

The little blond head of Henry emerged. He was gagging and choking. His arms flailed spastically as he struggled to get oxygen into his lungs.

Fred surfaced behind him. A big chunk of ice, a metre square, separated them. Henry began to sink under again, and he was just out of Fred's reach.

Lucky swam underneath the boy and pushed him to the shore. His mother and father and big brother pulled him out of the water and wrapped him in his father's coat. They rushed the little boy to the fire for warmth, as Paul worked on him and emptied his lungs of water.

The sounds of Henry coughing and vomiting were music to Bird's ears.

Lucky shook himself off, then ran to the fire to stay with Henry.

You're a good dog, Lucky!

I lost him, lost him. But I found him, found him.

Fred struggled out of the pond, after finding it difficult to get purchase on the frozen algae. Several people covered him with blankets.

He transmitted to Bird. *The boy's clothes were tangled in tree roots. He couldn't swim free.*

Bravo, Dad. You saved his life. Bird shivered with emotion.

No, Cody did. He'd already chewed through the roots by the time I got there.

Where is he?

I haven't seen him since he shoved the boy up from the bottom. Fred moved to the fire, dragging his blankets with him. *He saved the child. Sorry, Alberta.*

Bird couldn't take her eyes off the pond. Cody had still not emerged. *Cody? Cody?*

He was frail and old, and he hadn't recovered from being hit by the falling branch on Christmas Eve. That had been just the night before, Bird remembered, but so much had happened in the meantime that it seemed long ago. Bird feared the worst. Last night, she thought she'd lost him. She willed him to appear.

There was a slight disturbance on the surface of the pond. Bird leaned closer and held her breath.

The small grey body of an animal bobbed up limply.

Cody!

He didn't move. Bird waited for him to take a breath. He didn't.

Cody!

Nothing. No transmission and no movement.

Bird grabbed the rope that hung loosely from the rear of Cliff's truck. She fashioned a lasso and flung it into the water. It didn't reach. She reeled it back in and threw it out again, harder.

This time it encircled his head.

Cody began to sink. Bird pulled gently, and she felt the rope tug. She didn't want to strangle him, but she needed to get the animal out of the frigid water, and the sooner the better.

She stepped too close, and her legs slid on the algae into the water. She landed on her bottom but didn't fall in.

Bird steadily pulled him with great care, aware that she might lose him if she let the rope go slack. Parting the bobbing icy chunks as he came, Cody was finally close enough to shore for her to reach. Bird stretched her arms into the water and lifted him out.

He was lifeless.

Bird inhaled sharply. No! She wailed internally. No! Her head felt like it would explode. No! This cannot be true. Not Cody. No, no, not Cody. No.

She hung her head. Yes. Cody.

She needed to be alone with him, to have some private time to pay tribute to him in her own way, before others found out and flocked around. She kept her mind quiet.

Someone had dropped a blue blanket in all the fuss. She took it and wrapped the small coyote gently, and she held him in her arms as she sat on the ground.

There were many extraordinary animals in Bird's life, but this one held a place of special honour. He was exceptionally clever and intuitive. Cody had served his chosen people with diligence, bravery, and intelligence. He had never been domesticated. He chose where to live and what to do. He alone decided who to assist, who to protect, and when.

Bird knew that the first person he'd chosen had been Abby Malone. She'd found him as a sick pup and nursed him to health. They'd understood each other as much as people can who aren't able to communicate directly like Bird and Fred. Abby would be heartbroken at the news.

His last chosen person had been Mrs. Pierson. Bird smiled and wept at the same time as she thought of the little coyote curled up under Mrs. Pierson's blanket.

She felt a presence beside her.

"Hi, Henry," she said, without looking.

"Hi, Bird." He was quiet for a minute. "Is that Cody?"

"Yes. It's Cody."

"Is he alive?"

"No, Henry. He didn't make it."

The little boy put his hand on the blue blanket and left it there. "He came into the water, down where I was. He got the ropey things off that were holding me down. He's very strong."

Bird nodded. She noticed that Henry had changed from his wet clothes and now wore Spider-Man pajamas, under what looked like an adult's coat.

Henry continued describing what happened, tears streaming down his face. "I fell through the ice. I tried to get out, and I thought I was going up, but I was going down. Then Cody came, and then I don't remember." He sniffed and his whole body shuddered.

A woman stood behind them. She said, "Cody saved your life, Henry. He knew it might cost him his own, but he did it, anyway. That was the kind of animal he was."

Bird turned to see who had spoken. It was Henry's mother. The woman who had looked back at Sunny.

The young woman sat down beside them, and she put her arm firmly around Henry's shoulders. "Bird, you don't know me, but I admire you very much. Thank you for rescuing my son."

"But I didn't."

"You raised the alarm. Cody called you, and you made the rescue happen." Suddenly overwhelmed, the woman stopped talking. Bird knew what she was thinking. She was thinking that without Bird's special skills, no one would have known that Henry had fallen through the ice.

"My father would've heard Cody soon," said Bird.

Henry's mother looked startled. She wiped away her tears. "Every second mattered. Henry survived without any damage. I thank you." Her chin quivered as she spoke.

The reality of the woman's words sank in. Without quick action, it would've been a very different ending. "The temperature of the water worked for us," Bird said. "The colder the water, the longer the human body is able to live without oxygen. I read that."

The young woman nodded. "I read the same thing, and I was sure hoping it was true."

They sat quietly together. Henry's big brother, Luke, joined them, then their little cousin, Drake.

"Abby will have to be told," the woman said.

Bird nodded. "I know. She'll be sad."

"I'll tell her."

"Do you know her?"

"Yes. She rode my horse when I went away to school."

"Which horse?" asked Bird, mildly curious.

"The sire of your Sundancer."

Bird's heart felt like it had stopped. "Not … Dancer?"

"Yes, Dancer. She did really well on him."

"Yes, she did, I mean, I know, but …" Bird stared at this woman with new interest. "That means that you are …"

"I should've introduced myself. I'm Hilary."

"You're Hilary James? You're Mousie?"

She nodded and smiled. "I'm Hilary Casey now. Luke and Henry are Laura Pierson's great-grandnephews."

"Mousie. I don't believe it." Bird stared at her.

Hilary James was a legend. She and Dancer had ridden together and competed in some of the biggest, most prestigious horse shows in the world and won. They had even gone to England to ride before Queen Elizabeth, and the Queen had asked that Dancer sire a foal with her best mare, Casandra.

Bird was amazed. Mrs. Pierson had never mentioned a family connection. "How are you related to the Piersons?"

"Laura Pierson's maiden name is Casey. Her brother Henry was Sandy's grandfather. We named this guy after him." She ruffled the boy's hair with affection.

"I'm delighted to meet you." Bird meant it sincerely.

"We had Christmas with my mother, then when the highway opened, all the Piersons showed up to bring us here to be with Mrs. Pierson. All of us came but my grandmother, who isn't well. We left her there with her husband, Robert, and she's disappointed to miss this."

Mousie's grandmother was Joy Featherstone, and she and her husband owned The Stonewick Playhouse, which put on plays all summer. Joy was well known and loved in the community. Bird said, "I'm sorry about that. I hope she gets better soon."

"Me, too. She means the world to me."

While Bird and Mousie were talking, Henry had not taken his hand off the blanket. He felt it first. "He moved!"

Luke and Drake both put their hands on the blue blanket beside Henry's. "He moved!" Luke echoed.

Faintly, Bird heard a transmission. *Bird girl.*

Cody? Can you stay alive?

I can fight no more. It is my time. My body is weak and ready to rest.

Do you know how much you'll be missed? How much I will miss you?

I do.

Shall I bring you to Mrs. Pierson to say goodbye?

She knows already.

How?

The Good Man told her.

Pete?

Pete is here. Very soon, he will help me leave this earth and go to where I need to go.

Bird held him to her chest. She let out a muffled sob.

"What is it?" asked Mousie.

"Cody is dying. He is ready to go."

Henry threw his arms around Cody. He cried, "I'm sorry, Cody! Mommy and Daddy said not to, and I walked on the ice, and, and, and now you'll die." The little boy sobbed. "I'm sorry!"

Tell Henry I stayed here one more day to save him. Pete needed me to do this, on this Christmas night.

I will. Bird gently took the boy's hand. "Cody is glad that he could save you as the last thing he did, Henry. He is very old."

Henry wrapped his little arms around the blanket. Cody's nose wiggled out. He licked Henry's arm very softly.

Tell him this, Bird girl. It was meant to be. Do not be sad.

Bird nodded. "Henry, Cody says not to be sad. This is how it's meant to be."

"How did he tell you?"

"He told you himself, by licking your arm like that."

Henry accepted that it was true, because it was.

"Darlings," Hilary said, "it's a hard thing to understand, but every creature and thing that is born on the earth must one day die. Flowers die. Trees, birds, insects, animals, and people, too. We all must die."

Luke said, "Like your father died. With cancer."

"Yes, he did. A very long time ago. I still miss him."

"And the dinosaurs. They all died," Luke added. He leaned close to Bird, and confided, "Henry is very interested in dinosaurs."

Drake had been staring up at the sky. Now he pointed straight above them. "L-ook!"

They all looked up.

The sky changed for a brief moment. A purple glow swept over the moon, then swirled, becoming a rich pink tinged with blue at the edges.

Bird felt something else. A vacuum of sorts, like an uplifting in the atmosphere. And quickly, everything was the same again, like it never happened.

Except that Cody's life had gone from him.

From far away, she heard a deep voice with a smile in it. She recognized it. It was Pete Pierson's. It said, "Always choose kindness. The kind thing is the right thing. It's all about family."

Then he was gone.

Bird looked over to the fire where Mrs. Pierson sat on a lawn chair beside the fire, surrounded by her attentive sons and their families. She was looking straight up into the sky, just where Drake had pointed. Her entire face glowed with an inner, joyful light.

As Bird watched, Mrs. Pierson lifted both her arms to the sky and reached out, with her fingers fully extended. Then she blew a two-handed kiss to the heavens, and she brought her hands together under her chin, clasped in thanks.

What Bird had seen and heard by the edge of the pond, she would never forget. And she knew that Mrs. Pierson had witnessed exactly the same thing.

Sometime during Cody's death, Alec had come to sit with her. She didn't know how long he'd been there. He put his arm around her back. She rested her head on his shoulder.

Bird reflected on Pete's words. Mrs. Pierson lived by them, and she vowed that she would, as well.

Her devoted friend Cody was gone. Forever. His body was merely a shell that he'd used to contain his spirit.

Bird felt as empty as that shell, but she noticed that a seed of acceptance was beginning to grow. This was how it was meant to be, as Cody had said himself.

That didn't mean she wouldn't miss him terribly.

10 THE CIRCLE OF LIFE

And heaven and nature sing,
And heaven and nature sing,
And heaven and heaven and nature sing.

Bird hardly slept Christmas night. By the time she'd finally gotten to bed, she was too excited to relax. When she finally did, her sleep had been disturbed by random, vivid images of Laura Pierson lying helpless on her kitchen floor, Eva's face when she confronted Grandma Jean, and little Henry struggling under the ice. But it was Cody's heroic rescue and the price he paid that kept her awake. The loss of the small coyote was almost unbearable.

When Boxing Day dawned Bird felt horrible, convinced she was sick with the flu. She would stay in bed all day. She would never eat again. She opened one eye. Her cellphone read 6:55 a.m. She pulled the covers over her head and decided to remain there until she died of starvation.

But she had to pee. Badly. It could not wait. Groaning, she forced herself to get out of bed. On the way back from the bathroom, she couldn't help but hear the early chickadees singing outside her window. She put her hands over her ears to dull their cheerful sounds, but the plucky little birds reminded her of Laura Pierson and her indomitable spirit, and Bird began to feel the tiniest tinge of hopefulness.

Okay, she thought. Maybe I can live a little longer. There is some good in my life, she considered. Like Sunny. He loved to get in the ring and show off his stuff. They were already eager about next show season. And Alec. He was a really good thing in her life, and he was coming over later that afternoon for Cody's funeral. And her mother, Eva, was another, who for the first time had openly shared her past with her family. Her father, Fred Sweetree, and her little sister, Julia, who she loved so much, and Aunt Hannah and Uncle Paul, who were now happily married, and old Mrs. Pierson — all these people were really good things in her life. A smile tugged at her lips. Actually, there was much to be thankful for. Plus, she'd promised Amigo to begin his training today. She couldn't let the rescued horse down.

"Be brave and face the day," she said to herself aloud, but quietly, so as not to awaken the household. She pledged to enjoy this day, all day. "In celebration of Henry's dear life," she whispered, "and for my family and Mom, for Alec, for Mrs. Pierson, and especially in memory of Cody."

The sun wouldn't rise until close to eight o'clock, but the weatherman had predicted a glorious day. It would be too gorgeous to do anything but ride. She quickly got dressed.

The sky at the horizon was lightening, but it was still dark when Bird crept outside. The thaw had continued overnight, and the laneway was clear in patches. She expected that the roads would be the same. Her hope was to be gone before anybody was up, and she was impatient to jump into her saddle and take Sunny out into the woods.

All the horses in the barn greeted her with nickers. She reassured them that Cliff would be there on time to feed them, and she hastily tacked up Sunny. They were out of the barn before Cliff showed up.

I want double my breakfast when we get back.

I can't give you double, but I'll make it worth your while.

You better.

Stop grumbling, you miserable horse.

Bird and Sunny walked quietly past the house, careful to leave people sleeping. Bird didn't want Hannah running outside with a list of chores.

Once on the road the footing was good, so they picked up a brisk trot. She filled her lungs to capacity with the fresh, cool air, and enjoyed the freedom of stretching out and moving together with her horse after being locked in with ice. It felt so good.

The neighbours with their families had been gone by midnight the night before. Amazingly, even after her horrible experience in the ice storm, Mrs. Pierson was ready to stay up all night. She sure loves a party, Bird thought with a grin. In the end, her family had taken her home with them, including Mousie and the little boys.

Bird pinched herself. Had she actually met Mousie last night? The famous Hilary James? Yes. And they'd actually had a conversation. It was hard to believe.

Bird's mother, Eva, had become a little livelier as the night went on. Bird remembered their brief heart-to-heart and felt warm. It was a good beginning. And she was thrilled about the silver brooch with the rearing horse, Fred's gift to Eva on their first date. Bird was truly happy to own it. Before she'd gone to bed, exactly as she'd promised her mother, she'd put it in a special place for safekeeping.

Eva and Stuart had gone as soon as they knew that little Henry would be okay. Bird and Julia had walked them to their car. Eva had asked them to come with her to visit Grandma Jean, and both girls had agreed to visit her the next evening. Bird hoped that it would go smoothly. No matter what, they wouldn't give up. Grandma Jean was Eva's mother, after all, and their grandmother. Pete's advice about family and kindness must be followed.

Julia had stayed with Bird at Saddle Creek Farm. Hannah had insisted, knowing that Eva and Stuart needed some time alone.

Bird thought about Aunt Hannah and her new uncle, Paul. Around midnight, Bird and Alec had crept into the house and covered the newlyweds' bed with a million pieces of cut-up newspaper in place of confetti, and they had hung ribbons and Christmas bows randomly all over the bedroom. She chuckled as she imagined their surprise.

Alec had stayed until Aunt Hannah finally kicked him out, which was around 12:30 a.m. Bird felt a warm glow inside as she imagined his handsome face with his sparkling eyes and enchanting smile. They'd snuck in another few kisses before he left. Funny, she thought, how quickly time passes when you're with someone special.

Bird had no idea what time her father had disappeared. The last she'd seen him he was soaking wet, climbing out of the pond. Wherever he was now, Bird hoped he felt her love for him. She was resigned to the fact that she would only see him sometimes, whenever he showed up. That was enough. It had to be. She pressed her gloved hand over the necklace he'd given her, and she vowed to wear it always. One day he'd tell her about her grandmother. Bird wanted to know all about her.

Hannah, Paul, Julia, and Bird had cleaned up as much as they could and were in bed a little after 1:00 a.m. Cliff had made sure that the fire was totally out, and had hauled the straw bales back to the barn. He'd stored Cody's body, still wrapped in the blue blanket, somewhere safe until the funeral. The rest of the mess could wait.

Bird had wondered why the day after Christmas was called Boxing Day. She thought it was because there used to be boxing matches on that day, or that it was the day when people returned their presents — in boxes — to exchange for sale items or the correct size. Curious, she'd checked Wikipedia and read that the origin of the term was British, from the 1830s.

According to the *Oxford English Dictionary*, is was "the first week-day after Christmas-day, observed as a holiday on which post-men, errand-boys, and servants of various kinds expect to receive a Christmas-box."

It made enough sense for Bird to accept it as truth. The serving class got the leftovers. She hoped things had changed since 1830.

Low on the eastern horizon, the sun began to glow as they continued up the road. The ice on the branches dripped as it melted. The roads were all passable, and the air was chock full of singing birds, happy to have weathered the storm.

Bird wasn't unhappy, but she felt deeply that something was missing. That something was undeniably Cody. Until this day, even when he didn't show himself, Bird would sense that he was somewhere watching out for her, ready to warn her of danger or to head it off.

Today was very different. He was never going to pop his head up from the tall grass, or suddenly message her with a warning. It was hard to get her head around that fact.

Cody was gone. Not for today, but forever.

She missed his presence. But he still *had* a presence because she was thinking about him. Was it the lack of his presence that she was feeling? Or was it the reality of his absence, because in thinking about him she felt his absence?

You're driving me crazy. What the heck are you thinking about, Bird?

I'm thinking about Cody. I miss him.

I do, too. But all that absence stuff confuses me.

Bird grinned. *Me, too.*

They got to the T-junction in the road and turned left. Bird asked Sunny to walk for a bit. The shoulder of the road was soft with melted ice and mud, and Sunny's hooves sank deeply in some areas. She breathed in the fresh air and patted his neck.

Is there anything more glorious than a hack on a beautiful day? Bird asked.

Yes. Winning a trophy on a beautiful day.

You are the most competitive creature I've ever met.

You mean the most talented.

Bird laughed out loud. She found her horse hilarious.

They jumped a wooden coup fence from a standstill, then turned onto a trail up a rolling hill beside the woods. Once past some rocks, they began to trot.

A female deer was standing, alert, on the hill. Other deer would be hiding in the trees behind her, watching the horse and rider, and wondering if they were friend or foe.

We come in peace, transmitted Bird.

Yes, we know. You are Bird and Sunny.

Do you know us?

We see you often. You always come in peace.

Thank you.

Be safe.

Bird smiled. Animals know so much more than people think they do. They notice so much more, too, and people have no idea they're being observed. And they warn each other if there is something or someone to fear.

Bird's mind went back to the concept of the presence of absence. Pete Pierson had that effect on her. Suddenly, out of the blue, she'd have a strong sense of him. Like when he spoke to her last night. Did Pete really say that? Or was it a powerful memory of what Pete had been all about while he was alive? Kindness above all, and the importance of family, in good times and in bad.

Cody always used to say, "Take the good and leave the rest." Bird had thought that it meant you should eat the best part of a meal and throw the bad in the garbage, but he'd explained that it meant to let go of the bad parts of life and retain the good. She would try to remember that, too.

And what about her father? And Alec? They were alive, so it was different, but Bird thought about them a lot in very different ways when they weren't actually present. Both of them were present in their absence.

Stop doing that!

I'll try.

I'm going crazy here.

Then stop listening to my thoughts.

You're sitting right on top of me.

I'm not reading your thoughts.

Because you're too busy with this absence and presence, and goodness and badness stuff!

I'm just trying to understand things. When beings die, do they remain with us, somehow?

I'm not listening anymore.

Bird put those thoughts out of her head and concentrated on their beautiful ride through the pastures, past the woods.

They rode by some blanketed horses busily munching on a round bale in the fenced-off paddock. These were top show hunters, bred impeccably and trained to perfection. They looked serene and content in their herd, eating hay. Most show horses are isolated with very little turnout to prevent them from hurting themselves or each other. And when they kick up their heels, the grooms rush out to bring them back inside. Bird wished that all show horses would be allowed to hang out in such a natural setting as this.

Amen to that, messaged Sunny.

You said you're not listening anymore.

I will if I like.

Bird knew that Mousie had allowed Dancer to graze in a big field and to live like a horse. She had no choice, of course, because Dancer notoriously jumped out, anyway, but still, Mousie's philosophy was the same as Bird and Hannah's about the mental health of horses, and their need to buck and play.

And last night Bird had met Mousie in person. Bird shook her head in disbelief. After all the years of hearing stories about her exploits and great skill, Hilary "Mousie" James had become like a movie star in Bird's mind. A celebrity. But she'd been so very human, Bird remembered, when her little boy fell through the ice. And kind.

They entered the south forest from the edge of the hayfields at a walk. Sunlight speckled through the branches of the trees in the dense parts, and rendered the white snow blinding in the open patches.

Bird thought about her mother, Eva. Would this really be the start of a new and better relationship? Bird had been disappointed before. Time would tell. She must put bygones behind her, but recognized how difficult it would be to let down her guard. The pattern of their squabbles had been set long ago and would take willpower to change.

The childhood memories that Eva had spoken about at Christmas dinner were dreadful. Now that Eva had shared them, they weren't locked away in a box anymore, like Laura Pierson had explained, needing noise and movement and confusion to keep them hidden away. Maybe Eva would be able to examine them now, and put them in a perspective where they would be less harmful to her. And to the people around her.

Even though Bird had always suspected there was a reason that Eva was so messed up, this particular revelation had come as a shock. It was hard to imagine any father being capable of such betrayal, but if any father were, it would be Kenneth Bradley. Bird knew firsthand how selfish and conniving he was. He vindictively mowed down anyone in his way, including Bird, his own granddaughter.

After dinner last night, Eva had seemed much more thoughtful than usual. Giving Bird that brooch proved it. It was beautiful, she thought, but the meaning far outweighed the value. She couldn't remember a gift from her mother that was anything but clothes she would never wear or products that might improve her appearance, always given with an acidic barb that cut her down.

Bird sighed. Fred had said that Eva would need to do some hard work in order to begin to heal. Bird had no idea what that work would be or how long it would take. She promised herself that no matter what, like Mrs. Pierson had instructed, she would be supportive. She made a wish that Eva would be okay.

Well, she can't get worse.

Sunny, that's not very nice.

What? You forget so soon? She was horrible to you.

Okay. Maybe.

She messed you up, Bird.

But I'm okay now.

No thanks to her. She's selfish and unstable. Scary.

She's my mother. If I can help her, I will.

Aren't you the Miss Priss.

And aren't you the grinch who stole Christmas.

That's the second time you said that. What is a grinch?

I'll read you the book.

No thanks.

They reached a fork in the trail. One trail led more or less directly home, over a little wooden bridge and down a wooded path to the road. The other added fifteen minutes to the trip.

Bird felt a sudden, strong urge that she couldn't resist. She took the fork on their right and they headed west, the long way home through the woods. In these woods lived an assortment of wild animals, including many coyotes. In the past, Cody had been extremely watchful through here and a little tense until they'd passed safely through.

Again, Bird thought, I'm thinking about Cody. He indeed retained a presence in his absence, she thought.

Sunny threw his head up and down. He had something to say. *You confuse me, Bird. This talk about absence.*

I told you. I'm trying to sort out the whole death thing.

Animals are different than humans.

How so, Sunny?

We understand death. Humans don't. It's very simple. Before we are given life, we must agree to die someday.

Like a deal?

I guess so. At death, the deal is fulfilled.

Bird gave that some thought as they walked along. *This is helpful. Go on.*

Death is coming sometime, but we never know when.

And how do you get ready for it?

You cannot. If you think you're ready, you're fooling yourself.

Bird considered this. Sunny might be on to something. She had not been ready for Mr. Pierson to die, no matter how much she thought she was. And Cody, too. She knew he was old and not well, but nothing could've prepared her for his actual death.

And you think animals are better at this than humans?

Yes. We accept death. We mourn the loss of the spirit, but briefly, because we know there will be new life, which must agree to die sometime, too, before it's born.

And do you think of the lost spirits sometimes?

We move on. But we remember.

Sunny had given Bird a lot to think about. They walked along with no communication for a few minutes.

Then Sunny added, *I think of Cody, too.*

Yes. He was a remarkable animal.

I feel his presence.

Do you feel the presence of his absence?

I can buck you off at any time.

Bird laughed.

No, Bird, I mean it. I feel Cody's presence. Now. Here.

They trotted up along the fence between two properties, then cantered along a wide trail toward the old stone barn that had been converted into the Stonewick Playhouse by Mousie's grandmother and her husband Robert Wick. The playhouse was very busy during the summer, with plays in repertory, and left dormant for the winter.

Bird made the connection. Stone from Joy Featherstone, and Wick from Robert Wick. Stonewick. She'd never thought about it before.

The theatre was said to be haunted. Stories of Ambrose Brown's ghost had circulated for years. It was known that he always sat in a certain seat in the balcony of the theatre. Many people had seen him, including Abby Malone, who'd reported that he wasn't scary. Apparently he was very funny, but he had lived a sad life. Bird was curious to hear more details. She hoped to meet him one day. Maybe he'd talk to her like he talked to Abby.

Today the old place looked abandoned. She had met Joy only a couple of times, but the older woman had made a large impression on her, with her warm, intelligent sense of humour and caring, honest personality. Bird liked her a lot and hoped she felt better soon.

Bird smiled as she recalled the story of how Cody had led a pack of wild coyotes through the car of Samuel Owens as he was preparing to blow up the theatre, and how he'd blown himself up, instead. Owens's misdeeds were atrocious, and his demise was legendary. That night, Cody had become a local hero.

They trotted along the mowed path, past the theatre to the ditch, then up a rise with young fir trees on both sides.

Sunny suddenly stopped trotting. His entire body stiffened. He flared his nostrils and flipped his upper lip.

Bird.

What?

A very small animal is in distress.

Where?

Sunny looked to his left. He backed up. *Right there.*

Bird slid to the ground. She ducked under the low branches, getting soaked as they released their soggy icicles onto her bare neck and down the back of her coat.

Am I getting close, Sunny? I can't see anything.

One step more.

I see it.

There, down a hole in the snow, was a furry baby animal all curled up. Bird looked for any prints close by that might indicate that its mother was tending it, but she could detect no signs of activity around the hole at all.

Hello, little one. Can you hear me?

It made a tiny mewling noise.

Bird was struck by the helplessness of this creature, alone in wintertime. This day was mild, but cruel weather was sure to come back soon. It wouldn't live long out here.

Sunny, we're bringing him home.

Of course we are.

Bird broke away the crust of ice and lifted the tiny animal out of the hole. It had light grey fur and looked like a puppy. It was so young that its eyes were still closed. Bird stroked his cheek, and he snapped his tiny sharp teeth at her as quick as lightning.

She chuckled softly. *You're a wild little man. You're a baby coyote.*

Bird gently placed him in the large pocket of her winter coat, where he'd be safe and warm until they got home. Paul — Uncle Paul — would teach her how to feed him and keep him alive.

As she put her foot in the stirrup, she heard a transmission from far, far away.

Bird girl. A special present from me. To protect you.

Sundancer threw back his head and let out a long and hearty neigh.

ACKNOWLEDGEMENTS

A special thank you to Dr. David Goldbloom for making time to read this manuscript and for giving me guidance on the very sensitive issue of childhood sexual abuse. Dr. Goldbloom is a renowned psychiatrist and senior medical advisor at the Centre for Addiction and Mental Health (CAMH), and also a published author and Shakespeare scholar. He was my first choice as expert advisor, but I was reluctant to impose. I need not have worried. Immediately he wrote back with an open-hearted, generous offer of assistance, something he's done countless times for countless people.

My first readers are always my family, and a crucial part of every book I write. Their thoughtful reactions and acute instincts are invaluable to me. To my husband, my mother, my sisters, my children: I love you more than you'll ever know and I give you my thanks.

Marybeth Drake created the evocative and distinctive illustrations, and I am beholden to her once again. Thank you, dear friend.

I am grateful to the editors and publishers at Dundurn who launch my books into the world, and to my agent Amy Tompkins for her unfailing good advice.

Reference:

David S. Goldbloom, OC, MD, FRCPC

Senior Medical Advisor, Centre for Addiction and Mental Health (www.camh.ca)

Professor of Psychiatry, University of Toronto (http://www.psychiatry.utoronto.ca)